FIRE ON THE RIDGE

Other Apple paperbacks
you will enjoy:

Snow Treasure
by Marie McSwigan

Thank You, Jackie Robinson
by Barbara Cohen

The Mailbox Trick
by Scott Corbett

Sixth Grade Secrets
by Louis Sachar

The Hidden Treasure
(Hardcover title: *Tom Tiddler's Ground*)
by John Rowe Townsend

Radio Fifth Grade
by Gordon Korman

FIRE ON THE RIDGE

John Wells

AN
APPLE
PAPERBACK

SCHOLASTIC INC.
New York Toronto London Auckland Sydney

ISBN 0-590-43657-0

Copyright © 1989 by John Wells. All rights reserved. Published by Scholastic Inc., 730 Broadway, New York, NY 10003, by arrangement with Ashton Scholastic Pty. Limited. APPLE PAPERBACKS is a registered trademark of Scholastic Inc.

12 11 10 9 8 7 6 5 4 3 2 1   1 2 3 4 5 6/9

Printed in the U.S.A.   28

First Scholastic printing, March 1991

CHAPTER 1

The goat was more nuisance than it was worth. Every afternoon when Jason came home from school his first task was to take water to it where it was tethered, and sometimes Jason spent a weary half hour looking for it. This afternoon there had again been no sign of the animal. The stake was where he'd driven it into the ground. There was even a short length of rope, but no goat. He put down the bucket and made his way down into the gully.

"Never goes up the slope, does he?" Jason was talking to himself. "Never goes anywhere where it might be easy to find him. Always goes down into the thickest bush. Just a nuisance. No good for a single blasted thing."

Jason's dislike of the goat was a family joke. His father had brought it home to help keep down the undergrowth near the house. "He'll remove half our fire hazards. When this guy has eaten all the

1

rubbish under the trees we'll be safe as houses. Never get a fire through here after that." Dad had seemed so sure it was a good idea that no one had liked to argue about it.

"Fire hazards! It's all right for Daddy. I'm the poor silly fool that has to blunder around in the bush after the goat. And I think the goat is smarter than I am." He went on into the gully, mumbling and muttering to himself. He always felt better when he talked to himself. He knew that he could talk himself out of a bad mood. The others could laugh if they wanted to; it worked for him.

CHAPTER 2

When Shona arrived home, she fed the cats and the dog and went to her room to do her homework. It was easier to get it done before Mom and Dad got home. Once that was out of the way, she could do whatever she liked with her time, and what she most liked to do was to ride up into the town and out to the paddocks where her horse, Smoky, spent his days lazily eating grass. She didn't ride him much because he was now an old horse, but she'd learned to ride on Smoky and he'd become a good friend.

Whenever Shona had problems she could talk honestly about them to old Smoky. He couldn't answer but he always seemed to understand. He made Shona feel that she had a friend who was always on her side.

She spread her books on her desk and switched on her radio. She could just pick up some of the FM rock stations in the city and she liked to keep up with the latest hits. Her mother could never understand that you could concentrate on a radio and on your homework at the same time. You didn't listen to everything on the radio and you didn't really have to concentrate on all your homework, either. It was easy to keep up with your schoolwork if you didn't let yourself get behind, she thought. It was just a matter of staying on top of it.

The wind was whistling up into strong gusts and the noise it made in the trees all around the house began to annoy Shona. She closed all the doors and windows and switched on the air conditioner. That made more noise than the radio but Mom never complained about it. It was Mom's pride and joy and she ran it on days that were not really hot enough to need it.

Shona sat down and opened her books.

CHAPTER 3

There was no one else home when Kristian walked down the long, graveled driveway to his house. This was normal enough. Dad often didn't get home until well after dark. There were days when Kristian didn't see his father at all. It took a lot of money to keep the truck running and his Dad had to cart stone and gravel all over the place. He worked wherever the work was.

Kristian had no brothers or sisters and he was often alone. Mom played tennis three days a week and she'd often stop off at a friend's place for a coffee after the game. She didn't really like living here in the bush and it was good for her to get out and meet her friends.

There was no note about starting off the evening meal, so Kristian supposed that his mother would soon be home. He changed into his jeans and a T-shirt and went out to the shed. This shed held a wonderland of tools and machinery but there were two things Kristian prized above all others.

He had an old Yamaha trailbike there, and a brand new metal detector. He was determined to find gold and he didn't care how much everyone else laughed at the idea. An hour after he'd got home he was down in the bed of the creek, carefully passing the head of the metal detector over every drift of gravel, every crack in the ancient rocks of the creek bed.

CHAPTER 4

The three children had known each other in elementary school but now they went to different middle schools. Shona went to a girls' school in Kapana and the two boys went to school in Burke, a few miles further down the highway. They were in different classes and, though they were still friends whenever they met, they all knew that their friendship had weakened as they spent less time together. They were the only three children of their age group in the new streets on the western edge of the town and they still ran into each other often enough to keep in touch.

At six o'clock, Jason and Kristian were only about a mile apart in the bed of the creek. Jason had given up looking for the goat and was coming back to the house. He knew where the goat would be. Several times he'd come back from a lengthy search only to find it grazing happily near the peg from which it had broken free.

Kristian had found nothing. There had not even been a buzz from the metal detector in an hour and he knew that it was time to see whether Mom was home. Nearly snack time; time to go home. He started up the slope to the trailbike, annoyed at the heat of the afternoon and vaguely aware of the wind beginning to stir the treetops above his head.

The bush had been quiet when they all got home from school. The day was hot and the sky was a high, brassy color. The air was still and the trees hung their leaves like limp washing on a clothesline. The air was sticky and the flies walked on faces and arms and backs without ever flying.

Now the air was stirring and the wind was beginning to blow strongly, swirling and gusting down into the gullies. Both Jason and Kristian had their heads down, trying to keep the dust and grit from their eyes as they started home.

CHAPTER 5

Summer is the bushfire season.

When the blue haze rises above the hills in the heat of still, hot, summer days, the eyes of men and women living along the foothills turn unconsciously to the horizon several times a day. They are looking for smoke, looking for the smudge of a cloud that is not a cloud. Smoke is the bringer of evil, of death and destruction in the high summer.

For most of the year smoke means clearing land or the destruction of rubbish. In summer, smoke means bushfires.

Bushfires mean a wild savagery in the gullies and across the tops, through the clearings, over the farms and sometimes even into the towns. Everyone who grows up on the land watches for the smoke of the summer wildfires.

But there are people who come from the towns and in whose background there is no fear of "the red steer," no fear of the giant walls of flame that sweep the bushland or race through the summer-ready pasture, no fear of the bushfires. Sometimes these people do not watch for smoke. Sometimes when they do see it, it seems so far away that they need not worry.

Sometimes the bushfires catch these people.

This fire was to catch many people. Some of them would die. Others would be hurt. Many would lose their homes. It began as such a small fire. At first it didn't seem important.

It started in a paddock high on a ridge in the Dandenongs, a little below the ridge road and the new houses.

The fire spread slowly, as small fires in grassland usually will, unless there is wind. At first, the air was quite still. The wind came up later in the afternoon. People had seen the smoke by then but no one had worried. After all, it was a small fire and everyone thought that someone else would be doing something about it.

It was not reported to any fire department until two o'clock. At that time, the wind was rising far out over the western plains and great masses of air were beginning to move swiftly eastward. The winds were coming, and they were big winds.

The men of the Country Fire Authority knew the winds were coming. They knew that any fire at this time was dangerous, and this one more so than most. This fire was in the near hills and those hills were full of people. There were other fires in other places that day and the fire fighters were spread thin, doing what they could with what they had. No one could have done more, but it wasn't enough.

The fire was burning furiously when the first fire trucks arrived. In the few minutes it took to cut the fence and bring the two old trucks into the paddock, the fire reached the scrub and began to rise higher and higher as it clawed its way into the bush. The first scurrying gusts of wind were starting to move the trees and stir the flames.

The fire fighters called for help. When the next trucks arrived the fire was already off and running. More trucks were sent for and the afternoon heard the first of the sirens that were to wail all the long night. Only a hundred yards from the first houses the fire fighters took their stand. There was a track there, running right across the front of the fire, and this firebreak was their one chance to stop the flames.

That chance failed. The fire came to the wet and beaten grass and bushes and there it paused, but only for a moment. Water was thrown and pumped and sprayed. Beaters and rakes worried at the flanks and at the small feelers the fire put out across the dampened ground. For a brief moment it was stopped.

A gust from behind the flames picked them up and threw a great sheet of fire through the air, high over the heads of the fire fighters. A great wall of heat forced them to their knees, faces turned away. And then the fire was across the track and among the first houses.

These houses were empty. Police had already come along this track, with sirens calling and loudspeakers cutting through the hot, summer air, asking people to move out, away from the fire front, and the people had gone. Other things were burned, though. Clothes, pictures, souvenirs, photograph albums, carpets, curtains and toys; the fire took everything it could touch.

The wind was pushing the fire along hard now. Many houses were spared and many others were saved by heroic efforts. Some fire fighters fought for the homes of strangers while their own homes were burning.

The alarm was going out across the state. The big winds were pushing the fires along faster still and there were not enough trucks, not enough men, not enough water. Nothing would stop this fire now until it ran out of fuel. All the fire fighters could do was save homes where they could and then try to stop the flames when they again reached the open country.

Miles ahead of the billowing smoke, people were beginning to notice a change in the color of the sunlight. Where the sun's rays struck down, they tinged everything with a golden hue that might have been beautiful except for what it meant. There were those who knew and who began to prepare their defenses. There were those who thought that it couldn't happen to them. There were those who didn't even notice.

CHAPTER 6

The fire came from the south and the west. No one down in The Avenue knew it was there at first, but late in the afternoon a sudden spear of flame was flung by the wind across the hills and valleys in a narrow shaft that swept across the road which led south out of the town in the mornings and north back into it in the afternoons. This narrow strip of pavement was the town's main link with the outside world. When the road was cut, the little community knew that it was facing an emergency. A few hours later, they were to call it a disaster.

That sudden thrust of fire south of the town alarmed everyone but it passed and went stabbing into the country to the east in a narrow tongue of fire only a mile wide. It passed, but it left behind a few slower, smaller fires, deep in the timber. There were twists and trails of smoke coming gently up through the green masses of the treetops. The fire fighters were busy cleaning up the main fire and blacking out the burning posts and logs it had left behind.

The wind was still fitful and gusty and the day seemed to be growing hotter, though the sun had swung right over the sky and was close to the ridges now.

As dark fell it became harder, and then impossible, to see the smoke still gently rising from the trees. The flames had gone but the seeds of the fire still lived among the branches and the leaves, and the dry grass and twigs scattered on the forest floor. Small seeds of fire lived, and moved, and stirred. Small eddies of moving air crept among the trees, fanning this ember and that coal, stirring, blowing, gently fanning.

Over the tops of the trees the wind still rushed and roared in angry gusts but down under the canopy the air moved more gently, fanning, stirring, until small flames caught the edges of a leaf here, a blade of grass there. Small flames grew and reached out, seizing another leaf, a twig, a stick, some bark.

Small flames became large flames, taller than a man, taller than a house, taller than a tree, bursting through the canopy to suck greedily at the oxygen and the eucalyptus fumes, then exploding in a great sheet of fire right across the ridge. Suddenly, the whole hillside came to life with the hungry red flames. In a line they marched northward along the ridge toward the little township spread over the ridge and down into the gullies.

The fire fighters saw it coming but there was little they could do. Since that first swift sliver of flame had swept through to the south of the town, there had been a stream of emergency vehicles moving into the township along the smoke-darkened road. Police cars, ambulances, fire engines and tankers of every description seemed to be coming in a steady flood, until there was hardly any space left in the town to park another vehicle.

There was an army in place to fight the fire when it came to the township itself but there was no way to move that army to where the fire was striding up the hillsides and crawling down into the gullies. Nothing could be done until the fire reached the town, but by then it was too big and coming too fast.

CHAPTER 7

There were not many houses in The Avenue. It was still a new road, like a great scar running down the ridge and slipping off one shoulder into the long valley. There were more houses further up, but down at the new end, the low end, there were only a dozen houses, with three or four more being built.

Still, it was strangely deserted when Kristian rode up onto the pavement. There were many times when there was no one to be seen but there was always a sense of life in the place. Until now. Now the whole place seemed deserted, like a scene from a movie. It was a strange sensation and Kristian didn't like it at all.

He could smell the smoke, of course, but in summer there was often smoke in the air. It was nothing to worry about.

Jason, too, wondered where everyone had gone. He came up from the gully in a far happier mood

17

than before. Somehow he enjoyed his hunts in the bush for the goat, though he wouldn't admit it to anyone else. It was never quiet among the trees. He'd read somewhere that "among the trees, you can hear the earth breathe" and he felt a great sense of belonging to nature as a whole when he was alone in the bush.

Still, it wasn't normally this quiet.

Shona was the first to get an idea of what was really happening. She'd been working hard on her homework. She could understand the mathematics she was doing, but she had to work at it. She hadn't been listening very closely to the radio but when she stopped for a soda, vaguely surprised that no one else was home yet, she realized that the announcer's voice had a strained, excited tone to it. She flipped the air conditioner to a low setting and as the roar of the fans died away the sound of the radio filled the spaces around her.

He was talking about bushfires! He was talking to a reporter somewhere in the hills, and the reporter was shouting into the microphone. There was fear in his voice as he called out unbelievable details of giant flames leaping roadways, passing right over the heads of frightened motorists and fire fighters. And it was in these hills somewhere! The places he was talking about were places only miles away, off to the west! The fires were heading east! With this wind they'd come straight through the township. Suddenly, Shona was very frightened.

She knew what she had to do. They'd talked about all this before, but now it was hard to remember. What came first?

She ran out to the deck of the swimming pool, shocked by the hot, angry breath of the wind. It was making an appalling sound in the twilight, roaring through the trees above her head, thrashing them. Leaves and twigs, small pieces of bark, all kinds of debris went flying through the air. The pool was already covered with a scum of things blown from the trees.

And the smell! The smell of smoke was strong, a smell that brings fear to human and animal alike, for a fire is the oldest enemy of all. She knew that the enemy was out there somewhere, not far away, but she could see no glow. There was time, time to do all the things she'd been taught.

The house was already closed up because she'd had the air conditioner running and Dad would never let them run it with any doors or windows open. That was one thing. What else? And where was everybody? She could feel herself becoming very frightened. A large mass of something — fear? — was gradually filling her chest and her mind. She could actually feel it!

"Enough of that," she said aloud. "Things to do. Switch on, girl!" The sound of her own voice surprised her for a moment but it settled her racing brain. She began to think clearly.

Everything loose, everything that could burn, had to be put inside. The doormats, the pool equipment, toys, the washing off the line. She was running from place to place now, flying about the outside of the house. There might be very little time left. There might be no time at all. The curtains had to be drawn closed. Done. The cat was already inside. What else? There were a hundred other things and she couldn't remember them all!

Block up the spouts so they'd hold water. That was one thing. Getting onto the roof was no trouble and she stuffed all the drainpipes with towels. There were no leaves to clean out, because Dad had always been careful to follow the fire-season precautions. Run the hose onto the roof to wet it down and fill the gutters. What else? Wet down the walls. How much time? Was the fire really coming this way? What could she do? How could she fight it by herself? Where was everyone? She was beginning to panic, but she knew that she could not surrender to the fear.

The wind was blowing even harder now.

CHAPTER 8

Twice already the police car had come slowly down The Avenue, stopping at every house, warning people to evacuate. From their radios the police knew the whole picture and they knew The Avenue was threatened. From experience, they knew that it was better to leave than to risk lives for a few possessions. Houses and gardens could be replaced; lives could not.

There were people who didn't want to leave. They argued, and much precious time was lost. The fire was still coming and time was short. The wind was gathering speed and strength all the time and the heat was growing. Where there seemed to be no one at home, the police simply walked quickly around the house. If they saw no sign of life, they moved on to the next house.

Shona had not heard the car or the police knock on her door. The air conditioner was making too much noise.

"No one home," they thought, though it was strange that the air conditioner was running. The house was all closed up. They didn't hear Shona's radio. They moved to the next house.

Shona was left inside with her homework. When the police car moved out of The Avenue for the last time Jason was just coming up from the scrub. Kristian rode his trailbike on to the bottom end of the road as the police car turned out of sight at the top end. The three children were alone.

CHAPTER 9

Two and a half miles south of the town, on the edge of the scar from that first quick thrust of the fire, there was a roadblock. Only emergency vehicles were being allowed through. The commuters were coming home and by now they knew there was a big fire running wild in their hills. The smoke was clearly visible from the highway, boiling up into the sky and blanketing half the Dandenongs.

Men pleaded to be allowed through. Women wept with fear and frustration. The police were as gentle as possible but they held fast to their orders. The roads in the town were already choked with fire trucks and with people fleeing while there was still time.

An endless stream of cars came down that narrow road, moving slowly but steadily. A senior officer who'd just arrived at the roadblock could see the danger.

"It'll take only one car to break down, one person to panic, one car to have a fuel blockage, and that whole road will come to a halt. There'll be cars trapped between here and the town."

"It hasn't happened yet," said the policewoman he was relieving. "Mostly women drivers. The men are staying to fight or they're still at work. There hasn't been a problem on the road yet."

"You'd wonder where they all came from. I thought it was mostly bush up there."

"It still is, but there are houses everywhere in the bush now. I wouldn't like to live up there in bushfire weather!"

"No, and this is certainly bushfire weather! That wind must be up to ten or twenty miles an hour now. And the heat! Incredible! No wonder they can't stop the fire!"

"They won't stop this one. It'll go through the town like a bullet. The Country Fire Authority fellas reckon they'll stop it at the edge of the town but I don't like their chances."

"Well, I don't like this job either, but I'd rather be down here than up there!" He walked across to where another policeman was trying to tell a driver to turn off onto the side road and go back to Burke. "What's the problem, driver?"

"My kids are up there and I'm going up to get them!"

"You can't go up there, sir. Far too dangerous by now. The fire is already over the road on the other side of the ridge, and with this wind . . ."

"My kids are there! Let me through!"

"I'm sorry, sir." The policeman was being polite. "There isn't anything you can do up there at the moment."

"No, you don't understand. My kids get home from school about four-thirty . . ."

"Don't worry, sir, just don't worry. Everyone is being evacuated. There won't be anyone left up there but the emergency crews soon. Just turn down the side road there and go back to the recreation reserve. That's the evacuation center. I'm sure your children will be there by now."

"What if they're not? I want to go up and check for myself."

"I'm sorry, sir!" Anger was starting to color the policeman's voice. "You can't go up the road. You can see that it's too crowded with people coming out. Now move along . . . please."

"But you can't . . ."

"Move along, driver! Now!"

The car turned out of the line and went back along the gravel verge to the turnoff. The policeman began to explain the problem to the next driver. Already weary, he wondered how many times this scene would repeat itself. He understood how parents felt, separated from their children, but there was nothing anyone could do. The evacuation came first and any unnecessary vehicles going up the road would be a hazard to everyone.

"I'm sorry, sir. Only emergency vehicles are allowed through . . ."

Hundreds of people were evacuating the area in a steady, orderly flow. An evacuation and report center had been established by the State Emergency Service. Names were being listed. By morning it would be known just where everyone had been sent, unless the morning was too late.

The evacuation was going well, but no evacuation like this could be perfect. There were people who did not hear the warnings; people who did not have their radios switched on; people in houses tucked away where the patrolling police could not see them. There were people left behind; people overlooked and people who refused to leave.

In The Avenue there were three teenagers still wondering just what to do. Jason, Kristian, and Shona had not heard the warnings. The area had been reported clear.

"Well, as far as we can tell," said the two police. "You can't be sure, but there doesn't seem to be anyone down there now."

They were wrong, and the fire was coming quickly.

CHAPTER 10

Jason heard the trailbike coming up The Avenue even above the sound of the wind. He ran out to the side of the road, nearly tripping when a long strip of bark flying across the driveway wrapped itself around his knees.

"Hey! Kristian! Hey!"

The bike slowed, came to a halt.

"Jason! Where is everyone?"

"That's what I was going to ask you. There's no one around. And I can smell smoke. Heavy smoke! I think we've got a bushfire coming our way!"

"Yes, I think so too. But where are the fire trucks? Why isn't there anyone getting ready to fight it? What's happening?"

"I don't know. I'll put on the radio and see if I can pick up any news . . . why not ride that thing up to the town and see what's happening? There must be people up there! They must all be somewhere!"

"Hey, Jason, I can't ride this thing up to the town. It's not even registered. And I don't have a license. My dad'll kill me if he sees me on the road with it."

"But so what? There's something bad happening, Kristian. Something very bad."

"I know. I know there's a fire coming. But I'm staying. We've got a pump and there must be thousands of gallons of water in the pool. When it comes, if it comes, I'm fighting it!"

Jason remembered that Kristian had been like that in elementary school. He always saw things in simple terms. There were no shades of gray with Kristian. Everything was either black or white. He always took a straightforward look and stuck to it. You could never change his mind once he'd decided what he was going to do. Jason was more of a thinker and now he was thinking very quickly.

"All right. I agree with you. It looks as if we're on our own until someone comes, but we'd better plan what we'll do. We'd better think this thing through."

The two boys stood still for a moment, their bodies swaying slightly against the force of the wind. It seemed stronger out here on the road.

"Look," said Jason, "we'd better go up to your place. There is more cleared ground and you've got a gas-driven pump. Ours is electric and the poles won't last long in a fire, so we're going to lose power. You've got that big pool, too. We've only got the tanks, and the bush comes almost up to our house."

"Yes, but there are things you can do here, to . . ."

"I know. I'll get this place closed up and I'll wet everything down while we've still got power. I'll get everything I can save and I'll meet you at your place. Right?"

"All right, Jason. That makes sense. Do you think it's coming this way?"

"I know it is. I just know it is."

"Yes, I'm afraid you're right. In fact, I'm just afraid! There is one thing . . . how many other people are still down here? I haven't seen anyone at all."

"We've still got some time. Why not take your bike around the houses down this end and see for yourself? But be quick. I'll meet you at your place as soon as I can. We mightn't have very long to get ready!"

And the trailbike was gone, hardly heard above the rush of the wind. Jason ran back to the house. He knew all the things he had to do and he went about the tasks very quickly but very carefully. When he left he was carrying his schoolbag full of photograph albums and his parents' papers. He hadn't known what was important; he'd just scooped up everything that looked official. He'd looked for the goat but there was no sign of it. The house was closed up tight and there was nothing inflammable left near the walls to act as a fuse for the fire. The hose was left up on the roof, still running. Water was beginning to pour off the roof in a steady stream. And he'd only used fifteen minutes.

Kristian's house was a few hundred yards up the road and Jason was puffing hard when he got there. All the way, he'd been running with his load but he had kept turning his head to watch the western ridge. It was over there somewhere. That was where it would come from unless some miracle stopped it soon. No one was home at Kristian's house.

Jason began making the same preparations as he'd made at his own house. In a small part of his mind there was surprise at how much he remembered of what he had to do. He knew that he was doing a good job and even through the fear and excitement he could still feel pride. He hauled the heavy pump out of the shed and set it up beside the pool. He connected the delivery hoses and ran them out, one along each side of the house. He dropped the intake hose into the pool, but he was not certain when it came to starting the motor. Kristian would know all about that.

The wind had died a little and he heard the trailbike before it came into sight. Kristian had someone with him!

"Jason! We've got company and help here! Shona was home by herself too! And there is a man, Mr. Robards, coming down. He's wetting his place down now. He says he doesn't think the fire will come this way."

"I hope he's right but I don't think he is. Hello, Shona. Everything all right at your place?"

"Hello, Jason. Yes, I think so . . ."

"Well, let's get to it, Kristian, you start the pump. Shona, get hold of the hose on the other side of the house and spray the whole blasted place. Make a fire-break that is absolutely drenched. I'll take this one, Kristian. You start the pump and then set up some fuel. Then close up all your doors and windows . . . all those things!"

The pump roared into life and the hose became a live thing in Jason's hands. He began to sweep the stream over the roof and over the garden, wetting everything. There must be nowhere a spark could take hold.

The light was fading fast now and it was getting hard to see much. Jason wished that he'd brought a flashlight. Was that a glow in the western sky?

Just the sunset? Or something worse? The wind had died away again to almost nothing and Jason thought that the fire might be stopped now. If it stayed on the ground they could beat it. If the wind pushed it through the crowns of the trees there would be nothing they could do but take shelter. He looked carefully around for a place to hide himself if it came to that.

The carport had a brick wall facing the way the fire would come. That was the place to shelter. Jason remembered that radiant heat was the killer. You needed something to keep the direct heat off you.

Kristian came out of the house fully protected in long overalls. He had a "hard hat" and gloves on. Jason was already dressed in the right gear and he noted that Shona had herself well covered up, too.

Suddenly, there was nothing more to do. The place was as ready as it would ever be. The pump was switched off. They didn't want to waste fuel or water at this stage.

"What now?"

"Now we wait."

"I'm hungry, but I don't know whether I could eat anything," said Shona.

Kristian stood up. "I'll get some sandwiches or something."

"Sandwiches?" said Jason. "I'd like a three-course meal. It's way past my snack time and I'm hungry enough to eat a horse. With the harness still on it."

"I don't think I can eat," Shona said again. She was too nervous to want food. She knew that she should eat something while there was still time, but that was her brain talking and not her stomach. Her stomach felt like a tight little ball.

"Well, let's see what we can find. We have to eat." Kristian led the way inside. The sudden blaze of electric light made them screw up their eyes. "There'll be cans of things and there should be stuff in the refrigerator. There might not be much because Mom does her shopping tomorrow . . ." He stopped talking and turned to the refrigerator, stung by the sudden thought that he still didn't know where his parents had gone.

There wasn't much to eat but Kristian collected a variety of food. "I'll heat it all up. A good, hot meal will work wonders. You two could try the television to get some news; there must be something about the fire by now."

It was just as well that Jason and Shona went into the family room. They couldn't see what Kristian was doing in the kitchen. He opened a large can of baked beans and emptied it into a saucepan. It didn't seem to make much of a pile so he added a few things. Three onions were peeled and chopped into rather large and untidy chunks. A tomato was thrown in whole. It still didn't look like much food so he added the five eggs from the refrigerator door and roughly chopped up a quarter of a cabbage. He added a can of cream of mushroom soup and a little water; that filled up the big saucepan rather well.

He also turned the burner onto "High" to save a little time and, after giving the mess a quick stir to mix things up a bit, he went into the family room to join the others.

The result was predictable and quite horrible. The heat was far too great and the whole mass stuck to the bottom of the saucepan and began to burn. Within ten minutes the kitchen was filling with smoke. Shona smelled it first and came rushing out to scoop the saucepan off the stove. "Kristian! Look at this. You've ruined it!"

Jason looked curiously into the saucepan. "I think it was ruined even before it was burned," he said. "What was it before Kristian wrecked it?"

"That," said Kristian proudly, "smells as if it's about ready to eat. I call it . . ."

"Don't call it anything! My mother always says that if you can't say anything nice you shouldn't say anything at all. And there isn't anything nice you could say about this!"

"Being a little burned will give it a nice, nutty

flavor," answered Kristian. "You'll love it." He stopped any further argument by filling three large bowls with the nearly solid mess and handing out spoons.

The three ate. Kristian finished his and had a little more, scraping it from the bottom of the pot, but he might have just been trying to prove that it was edible. Jason ate half of his and then gave up.

"It's very filling, Kristian, but that's about all I can say for it. What's this?" He was fishing something like a large piece of seaweed from his plate.

"That's cabbage of course, very good for you."

"It might have been cabbage once, but it isn't now. Cabbage is green and tastes like . . . like cabbage. This is brown and doesn't taste like anything at all!"

Shona was only picking at her food. "I think I've got a chunk of egg here . . . and these look like baked beans . . . I think."

Kristian knew they were joking. It wasn't a good meal, but it wasn't all that bad, either. Secretly, Kristian was rather proud of his effort. He'd never cooked a meal before. "I have another course ready, anyway. You don't have to eat all that. Unless you want to, of course . . ."

Jason and Shona looked at each other and pushed their plates away. Kristian merely went to the cupboard and came back with a large piece of cheese and a length of thick, brown sausage. He cut slices off each and arranged them on a plate. "This is our dessert. Dad loves this. It's very tasty."

"And smelly." Jason was looking rather strangely at the plate, but he took a piece of sausage and put it on a slice of cheese. "Still, we'll need to have eaten." The cheese was a strongly flavored and rather hard-to-chew type, and the sausage contained many spices, including coarsely ground peppers, but they managed to eat most of it without offending Kristian. It was like nothing that Shona or Jason had ever eaten before. Kristian ate huge amounts of both and gave every appearance of enjoying it enormously.

"These are Dad's favorite foods. He makes the sausage himself. Takes all day. Smells the place up something shocking, but it tastes good." He was chewing mightily while he spoke. "I'm not usually allowed to eat too much of it. Dad keeps most of it for himself and for whenever we have guests."

Again Shona and Jason exchanged looks, but neither of them said anything.

Kristian made coffee, with plenty of milk and sugar. That was good and they each had two large mugs of it.

"What did you think?" asked the would-be cook. "Had enough?"

"Well," said Jason, "I enjoyed the coffee . . ."

"And the cheese wasn't all that bad." Shona was trying to be helpful.

"Glad you liked it," said Kristian cheerfully. "We'll just leave the dishes until later."

They moved back to the television set. There had been nothing about the fire when they'd looked before but now every channel was carrying reports. There were large fires burning in three different areas of the state. In one place, the people of a beachside town had gathered by the water as their town burned. Every channel carried pictures of the fires crawling down gullies, exploding across ridges, sweeping through paddocks of grass, devouring and destroying homes. The three teenagers said nothing. There wasn't anything to be said. It seemed that half the world was on fire.

Kristian jumped up and turned the set off. He turned to face the others and he hoped that he didn't look as frightened as Jason and Shona looked. "There was nothing there about this place. It didn't say anything about this town. That must mean we aren't in any real danger."

No one argued, but no one believed what he said, including Kristian. "I wonder where our families are now?" Shona asked.

Later the three stood in the darkness watching the ridge. The sky was red now and in the glow that was coming from the west they could clearly see the smoke coiling and writhing up into the night sky. The fire was still alive and it was coming. The wind was getting up again but as yet it was gentle, barely moving the trees. There had been no wind for the past hour but they had been too busy to notice the eerie stillness and now it was gone.

"I tried the telephone. It's gone. The wires must be down somewhere." As Kristian spoke the light pouring from the windows of the house suddenly blacked out. "The electricity has gone out now."

"Good job we didn't stay at my place, then," said Jason. "Our pump's electric. It wouldn't be any use at all."

"Good thing we found each other. I wouldn't want to be home alone, just waiting for something to happen. It's bad enough even with company," said Shona.

Jason smiled at her, though in the gloom a smile was hard to see. "You're right, Shona. It isn't any time to be alone. I'm glad you're here."

He was looking out to the west, through the darkness. Shona couldn't see his grin but she could hear it in his voice. She suddenly felt a little better. What if they were only kids? They'd been taught what to do if a fire came their way, and they'd done it.

"You mean you think cooking is woman's work? To a man, everything seems to be woman's work.

Call yourself the stronger sex? Hah! I've done just as much fire fighting as you have, Kristian!"

"That's only because none of us have done any real fire fighting at all, Shona. So far we've only been getting ready, and waiting." Jason was the cool one, the thinker, but Shona wished that he'd kept the joking going a little bit longer. That small joke about woman's work had made her feel much better than all the preparations they'd made so far.

"Hey, Jason, don't be so serious." Kristian had obviously thought the same thing as Shona. "Think of this as an adventure. We could play our tapes and our records as loudly as we liked, if we wanted to. The neighbors wouldn't mind because they've all gone. Of course, having a little electricity would help . . . our tape deck doesn't have a pedal generator!"

Shona picked up the mood again. "We could just ignore our homework . . ."

"I have already," said Kristian.

" . . . but I've done mine!" wailed Shona.

"I don't think any of my teachers would accept a simple thing like a bushfire as a good enough excuse," Jason muttered. "An atomic bomb might just do it."

The serious moment was past. They were all joking again. Things felt better. Beneath it all, the three knew there were serious times ahead that night but, for the moment, a little humor helped.

"If it comes to that, I could probably do a lot better with a meal than you did, Kristian! Maybe cooking is woman's work after all. I can still taste that sausage! And the cheese wasn't much better!"

"And I," said Jason, "am still trying to digest it all. I can taste it and I can feel it. My stomach feels as if I've eaten razor blades and broken bottles."

"Get off my back," Kristian laughed. "I know it wasn't much of a meal, but it'll keep you all going. I never said I was a good cook!"

"A good cook? A good cook? I wouldn't have said you were a cook at all. I've had better meals when I haven't had a meal at all!" Jason was back in a good mood.

"That," said Shona, "was a Clayton's meal."

"And just what do you mean by that? It has to be a vicious attack on my cooking!"

"Well, a Clayton's meal is the meal you have when you're not having a real meal at all."

"Very funny. Very funny indeed. You can cook breakfast, just for that."

"Thank goodness," Jason laughed. "I was wondering what masterpiece you'd produce for breakfast. Ice cream with tomato sauce, perhaps. Or sardines and watermelon."

"Well, I hate to break up this happy little discussion of my great ability as a chef but I think we'd better give everything another wetting down.

With this wind building up again things will dry out quickly."

"Good idea, Kristian. You and I can do that while Shona washes the dishes! That's 'woman's work,' isn't it?" Jason was smiling while he said it and they were all smiling as they set to work.

CHAPTER 11

"Hey, kids! Everyone all right down here?" There was a man walking down the slope through the trees, a shadowy figure in the evening gloom. The three peered through the twilight until he came closer. It was a middle-aged man, dressed rather carefully in new overalls and with workboots so clean they shone even where there was no light at all.

"I know him," said Kristian softly. "Mr. Robards. Odd guy. Lives up the road a way."

"You kids all right here?"

"Yes, yes. We're fine. And we're ready!" Somehow, Jason saw the man as an intruder. He'd come to think of this as their own fight. They'd seen no one else since they got home. The whole street had been deserted, or so it seemed. Now here was this man walking through the bush to them as though there was nothing wrong at all.

Shona spoke. "Where is everyone? Why isn't

there anyone about? What's happening?" Jason gave a little start when Shona spoke. She'd been very quiet, doing what had to be done without saying much. "Do you know what's going on?"

"Yes, I'm afraid I do, and it isn't very good news. The fire is out of control. Moving very fast. I think it is coming this way still. I might be wrong, but I don't think so."

"Where are the fire fighters? Why isn't anyone down here?" Kristian wanted to know. The arrival of this man had reminded the children just how alone they were. Until this moment they'd been too busy to think much about it, but now the silent bush and darkened houses seemed threatening, far worse than the danger that lay somewhere over the hills.

"There aren't enough fire fighters, son." Both Jason and Kristian hated being called "son." "There are four or five big fires. Everyone's flat out. But how is it that you're still here? This area was evacuated, cleared out, hours ago."

"We didn't hear anything. No one told us anything."

"You can still get out. The road up to the town from here is still open, but I don't know . . . you might not be any better off up there. We just don't know where the fire is going to hit us. It might be up the side of the ridge and it might miss us altogether. It's a question of where do you run to. I don't think that up there is any safer than down here."

"I'm not leaving. This is my home and I'm staying right here! We're ready for this fire, and it isn't getting my house!" The anger was raw in Kristian's voice.

"Take it easy, son. I'm not asking you to leave and I don't have any right to tell you what to do. I'm just checking down this way to see if there's anything I can do to help. Any animals needing to be set free. Anyone left behind. That sort of thing. What you choose to do is your own business. But I may be able to be of some help."

The three youngsters relaxed a little. All three were thinking, surprised at how they'd already come to think of themselves as a heroic little team, ready to battle a giant. Yet all three knew that this could be a dangerous way to think. They might end up needing all the help they could get.

"Thank you, Mr. Robards. We were just a bit surprised to see anyone. We thought we were on our own." Shona was always the first to remember her manners.

"Understood, understood. Do you all know what to do? Have you got the place ready?" Jason noticed that even as Mr. Robards was speaking his eyes were running all over the place. He wasn't missing a thing.

"We think we're organized. Can you think of

anything we've missed?" asked Jason.

"No, not really. You've got water. Pump working well? No, you seem to have everything ready. There is one thing I want to say, though . . . stop looking so annoyed with me, son. I'm not trying to boss anyone around. Do you know much about the way a fire behaves?"

"No," said Kristian. "We aren't experts. We never said we were."

"There aren't any experts at this sort of thing, son. Least of all me. But I see that you've got both hoses running out toward the front of the house. It's all clear up the front. You've got the driveway, the parking spaces and the street itself out there as a firebreak. There isn't much in the front garden to burn. I'd bring at least one hose, and probably both, back here. That's a pretty dense gully down there, full of fuel for a fire. It runs uphill to the house and a fire travels faster uphill. If it comes up this way you'll need a lot of water out here, and quick smart too."

"That makes sense, Kristian. Bring your hose back, Shona. Lay it out around the end of the pool, but not out in the open. We don't want the hose itself being burned. And make sure there aren't kinks or twists in it." Jason heard himself giving orders. Was he trying to show this man that he knew what to do?

"Good thinking, son."

The man walked off a short distance, then he stopped. "I'm going on down to the bottom of the road. I'll be back shortly, when I'm satisfied there isn't anyone left behind. OK?"

"OK," said Kristian. "We'll see you on the way back." He saw Jason looking across at him. "Well, he was only trying to be helpful. I just don't like being called 'son.' What he said made sense, though."

Shona spoke from the darkness where she'd been laying out her hose. "There is something we've forgotten, and that man didn't mention it, either. What about radiant heat?"

"Radiant heat? I think we'll be warm enough, Shona!" It was Jason's first attempt at a joke for a long time.

"No, be serious. It is radiant heat that kills most people caught out in a fire, you know. That's why we had to close the curtains. They stop the heat getting onto the carpets and furnishings and things. That's why you get down on the floor if you're trapped in a fire in a car."

"OK, that's all true," said Kristian, "but we've closed the curtains and we aren't in a car. What are you getting at, Shona?"

"Well, we have to have somewhere to get away from the direct heat in the first few moments. If the fire comes this way there will be a wall of heat, sort of, in front of it. That will be the hottest part.

We'll have to get out of the line of it. We'll need something to get behind until the worst of it passes. They say you can get out after the front passes and then put out anything that has started to burn. I read it somewhere . . ." Her voice trailed off as she realized that she was talking about a terrible possibility. This was no game.

"She's right, Jason. We should be able to keep the flames away, but that isn't the same thing as protecting ourselves from the heat."

Jason was thinking. "Makes sense. I was thinking about that before. The problem is that we don't know which direction it might come from. We'd better work it out. We've got the pool, and the carport has a brick wall . . ."

"The house is a firebreak itself. We could get around the house, or shelter behind the brick wall in the carport. We should have time to tell which direction it comes from." Shona was almost wishing that the fire would come now so they could get it all over and done with.

"OK, here is what we'll do." Jason had somehow become the leader. "We will walk around the house now, calmly, and we'll fix in our minds all the places we can hide from all the different directions. We'll go slowly. We'll all tell each other what we see and we'll all have it fixed firmly in our minds. There might not be time to look around later on."

They did that. They went slowly and looked at the earth banks and the brick walls. They considered the pool and they looked at the garden shed. No one pointed out that there was hardly enough light to see. If they needed to take shelter too quickly it would be because there was too much light, the great red and yellow light of a bushfire.

The other strange thing was that none of these children had ever seen a bushfire, yet each held in his or her mind a picture of just how it would be. When it came, it was far worse than they could have imagined.

CHAPTER 12

Mr. Robards was back when they'd finished their inspection. He came out of the darkness while they were comparing their ideas.

"Hello again! Any news?" His voice was so calm that Shona thought that he must have been keeping himself very carefully under control. It was either that or he didn't think there was any great danger.

"No, no news, and no sign of anyone else. Did you see anyone else?"

"No, we're all alone down here. I heard a motor a little further up the slope about an hour ago, though, so there must still be people up there. We won't be alone if it comes this way."

No one spoke, and he went on. "Well, there is one thing I have to ask you. I know you've done everything you can here, and I'm certainly not trying to take over, but I have to ask you this. Are you determined to stay? Do you want to come a little further up the road? It's your decision."

There was another small silence, then Kristian spoke. "We thank you for coming down, Mr. Robards. We appreciate your advice. But this is where we planned to stay and, until our folks come home, this is where we will stay."

"I understand. You might be making a big mistake, but then again, you might not. No one really knows which places will be safest. I'll come back down later and see how you're doing . . . if that's all right?"

"Of course. Thanks. We'll be fine. We'll see you in the morning."

"I hope so, kids." As he walked off up the road they could hear his footsteps on the gravel, slowly fading into the night. In the silence they felt more alone than before.

"No wind. The wind has gone again." Kristian had his face turned to the sky. "The wind has stopped altogether."

"Doesn't mean it won't be back," Jason said. He didn't want any hopes raised too soon.

"Listen!" Now it was Shona. "Can you hear the sirens?" In the still, warm night the children could faintly hear the sirens as fire trucks and police cars, ambulances and tankers filled the distant highway.

"Those sirens mean that they all think the fire is still coming." Jason's voice was flat. He was already tired and already afraid. He knew that the fear was still growing in him and he tried to push it back out of his mind. It wasn't easy and he didn't quite succeed.

"Ohhh! Look at that!" The night sky was suddenly lit by a rich yellow-orange glow right along the ridge to the west. The light was so strong that it shone on their upturned faces. The trees could be seen now. The sky was a great rising, twisting mass of yellow cloud, lit from underneath. The clouds seemed to be moving over them, filling the sky with an evil menace.

"Well, now we know. It is still coming. And it's coming here." Kristian's voice was soft. None of them had ever seen a sight like this before.

"Keep calm, everyone. We know what we've got to do. We know where to shelter. Just wait, now, and keep calm." Jason was also talking softly, calmly. Strangely the fear was beginning to leave him now. At least they now knew that it was coming and at least they knew where it was. "Until this moment," he thought, "the fire had been like a strange, silent monster creeping through the dark. We didn't know where it was, what it was doing. Well, we know now, and we're ready for it."

A ribbon of gold outlined the ridge with a line of bright, pure color.

"It's beautiful." Shona's voice held wonder in it and what she said was true. That line of light had an eerie magnificence.

The moment lasted a few seconds and then the

ribbon of light spilled over and down the slope toward them, running down it like a liquid, faster here, slower there, coming down the slope in a ragged line. They could see the outlines of the trees as the fire reached them.

"It's on the ground! It isn't in the tops! We'll beat it!" Kristian spoke with a terrible determination. Jason looked across at Kristian. At that moment the light striking his face made him look like a grown man.

CHAPTER 13

"A little time yet, Shona. Unless the wind gets up, we've got a little time yet. Start the pump, Kristian. Make sure it's fueled right up."

Kristian just smiled. "Relax, Jason. That ridge is two miles from us. And the pump is fueled up. It'll start first try. I've even got spare fuel and you'd never guess where! The drum is in the pool, with the top screwed down very tightly. The fire won't find it there! This rope goes to the handle, see?"

"How long will a tank last?"

"I don't know. A fair while, but we've enough fuel to keep it running all night, if we have to."

"I'd be happier if we had it running . . . just in case it doesn't want to start when the time comes."

"No worries, mate. It'll start, but I'll get it going now just in case."

Kristian was right. The pump started first try. Jason and Shona took up their hoses and they could feel the water rush down to the nozzles, filling the hoses and making them hard. They began wetting everything down again; the roof, the grass, the shed and the bushes.

"That'll do for the moment, Jason. We can't waste the water!" It was a big pool but it was all they had. Without electricity there was no way to get at the water in the house tanks. The two hoses were closed off but the motor was left running.

CHAPTER 14

For the next half hour there was very little to do but watch the flames come slowly closer. The wind had died away again to almost nothing and the fire was barely moving at all. They could hear it snapping and crackling among the trees and the dark scrub but there was little to see. The lips of the fire had passed down the ridge to the west and into the deep gully below, out of sight. There were a few trees burning on the ridge but it was nearly all in darkness, with just a red flare where the bark of a tree or a fallen log still smoldered.

"It doesn't look too bad now, Jason."

"No, it doesn't. We'll be all right if the wind doesn't come up again. If it does, though, we'll be showered with sparks here. You'd better keep everything wet. Shona, could you have another look around? See that everything burnable that can be moved has been moved inside. Into the house or the shed, it doesn't matter which."

55

"OK, Jason. You make that pump work hard when we need it, Kristian. I'm getting a bit scared again. I wonder whether we should have left while we could . . ."

Jason reassured her, though in some ways his words weren't very reassuring. "It's like Mr. Robards said, Shona. We might be as safe here as anywhere else. Remember that the town is on top of a steep ridge and fires burn much faster uphill. If the wind gets up again I don't think the town will be any place to feel safe."

Kristian moved slowly around the house, spraying water everywhere. The spouts were overflowing and there was water running down the gravel driveway. Even the cleared, grassy area between the house and the bush was drenched. A wide sweep of the hose caught Shona and Jason where they stood talking. They were soaked.

"Hey! Cut it out! That water's cold!" Jason sounded quite angry.

"Sorry," called Kristian, in a voice that didn't sound as if he was at all sorry, "but you told me to wet everything down. Everything. That includes you two! Just doing my job! And it'll stop any sparks catching in your hair."

Shona shuddered. "I wish you hadn't said that, Kristian."

"Sorry, Shona. Didn't mean to frighten you." This time he did sound sorry. "When the fire gets here you might be better off inside. There are only two hoses for the pump so we don't really need a third person out here."

Before Shona answered a new sound came to them. It was a distant roar, a loud but faraway sound. It wasn't the fire. They all turned to the west, listening, straining to understand this new sound. The trees sprang to life overhead as the first gusts ran through them. The wind had swung around a little and now it was coming back, even more strongly than before!

"Here it comes." Jason spoke quietly but they heard him with a dreadful clarity. "Up the back gully. We're in for it now! Remember what we all have to do!"

A yellow-gold light shone up the gully between the trees, but for a moment there were no flames to be seen. The first small, bright fingers of flame crept into view, growing stronger, bolder, as they watched. Within a minute, the bottom end of the gully was full of light and flames were visible between the trees. Another roaring gust of wind rushed through the treetops and suddenly the whole gully was full of fire.

The three teenagers didn't see the fire rush up the gully because they'd turned their faces away from the wind's fiery breath. When they turned back to face the enemy they saw a terrible scene. Where the bush had been black, with just a glow from the gully, there was now a raging bushfire spreading for hundreds of yards up the hill. The main thrust of the fire had gone up the gully, where the hills had funneled and channeled the wind, missing the house, but now the fire began to spread sideways, to climb up out of the gully and march toward the house. Jason saw Kristian step down from the poolside decking and drag his hose toward the fire.

"Kristian! Kristian! Come back up here, Kristian!" Jason's angry shouts were lost in the wind and the huge sound of the fire. "Shona, grab this hose and watch for sparks that catch! Get onto them straight away!" He ran around the pool, his arm over his face to keep away the terrible heat. He raced along the line of the hose to Kristian, where he stood grimly waiting, playing the arc of water back and forth.

"Kristian, get back! You're in the edge of the trees! You can't fight it here! It'll go over the top of you! Get back into the clearing."

"It's coming up here, Jason. I'm ready for it! Just let it try to get past me!"

Jason could not make him come back. The heat was so strong now that he could barely look into the gully, down the slope towards the advancing flame. Kristian must come back! He'd be badly hurt, or worse, if he stayed among the trees. Jason ran back to the pool deck, seized Kristian's hose and gave it a mighty tug. Kristian spun around with the sudden pull and fell to his knees, the hose jerking free.

Jason dragged more of the hose back and Kristian had no choice but to scramble to his feet and follow it. He caught up to the nozzle and pounced on it. He and Jason then had a grim tug-of-war but Jason was stronger and Kristian could not get back down the slope.

"Now, Kristian! Behind you!" Jason flung out his arm to point and Kristian saw him clearly. The light was strong now, the yellow, red, white light of a bushfire in full cry. The flames were at the edge of the trees and coming out onto the grass. Kristian swung his hose to the edge of the fire and began to play it backward and forward, cutting off the advance. Jason watched him for a moment, then ran back to where Shona stood near the house, holding the other hose.

The wind was roaring nonstop in the trees and the few small gums near the house were thrashing from side to side, twisting and turning as if they, too, sought to escape the fire's hot breath. The air was almost too hot and dry to breathe but they all had damp rags across their mouths and this helped. Sparks flew through the air and the fire itself sent long streamers of flame out across the ground like snakes, writhing and turning this way and that, always looking hungrily for fuel.

In horror, Jason saw that fire was heading up the gully across the road, parallel to the gully behind the house. They now had fire on three sides of them and at the rate it was moving they'd soon be surrounded. What to do? What move to make next? Even as Jason was thinking he was also feeling anger. This was not something he should have to organize. Where were the adults? Where were the fire fighters? Why had the three of them been left to face this alone?

"Shona, you take this hose and stay out in front of the house. Keep that bark and other stuff wetted down. Don't let that fire come across the road!"

"Jason, I don't think I can . . ."

"You can! You've got the road to protect you and there isn't much fuel there anyway! Just don't waste the water. Kristian is going to need all he can get." Jason ran back to see what was happening on the rear slope.

He ran back down the line of the hose to Kristian. He had to bend nearly double as he ran because great sheets of flame-ridden smoke were sweeping up the short slope. The smoke was burning in his lungs and tears poured from his eyes. He found Kristian bent low over the hose, playing it left and right, left and right, sometimes doubling back to wet down a stubbornly burning spot.

"Doing well, pal. Doing well. Keep it going."

"Hey, hello! Didn't see you there. You're rather

well hidden in all this smoke. You've gone a sort of sooty color. How's the level in the pool?" Kristian kept playing the hose as he spoke.

"No worries! Hardly gone down at all! Can you hold it along this side?"

"I think so. It'd help if I could go in after those spots that keep flaring up. I've got a band of burned grass there as a firebreak now but I keep getting sparks blowing back up here in showers. Every spark that lands seems to start a fire. I'm keeping up with it but that's about all. If we run out of water I'm in real trouble, Jason!"

Jason was already gone, back into the smoke.

He checked on Shona, but she had no problems. The wind was taking the fire away from her and she was keeping up with the sparks and burning leaves blowing over the house from the gully behind. "Keep the roof wet, Shona!"

"Will do! How's Kristian doing?"

But Jason was already gone.

Back beside the pool he felt eyes looking at him. He had that strange sensation of being watched. He looked around carefully but there was no one. Wait! There was a sudden, short movement in the darkness between the end of the pool decking and the shed. What could it be? There was no one else around.

He crept closer, wishing that he had a flashlight. This was very strange. He stood as tall as he could, peering into the darkness, and he saw the movement again. Wallabies! There were two wallabies sheltering behind the protection of the pool wall, on a wet patch of grass. They watched Jason with no fear. They knew that the fire was their enemy, and they had no fear of the humans who were fighting it.

Jason was delighted. He loved the animals of the bush and several times through the evening he'd had to block out thoughts of what the fire must be doing to the wildlife. Here, at least, were two animals that would make it safely back into the bush when the danger was past.

This would be something to talk about afterwards, but "afterwards" was still a long time away, he knew. As it happened, he didn't get a chance to tell anyone about the wallabies that night. It was to stay as one of his memories, one of the things he'd carry in his mind forever, bringing it back to the surface whenever this dreadful night came back to him. It was a positive thing, a good thing, and there had been very few of those.

He took a bucket from near the pool and filled it with water. No one saw what he was doing. There were only two other people to see, and they were busy. He ran awkwardly down the slope to the edge of the flames, squatted for a moment and, peering under the smoke, he could see three spots where heavy stumps were burning. They were the ones throwing up the sparks that were troubling Kristian. He took a deep breath and plunged into the smoke, pushing his way blindly forward, eyes almost completely closed. He found the first stump and poured the bucket of water over it, killing most of the flames and the coals.

There was no time to see what happened. Still holding his breath, his ears roaring, he staggered back up the slope, through the ashes of the long grass at first and then onto the shorter grass of the clearing. He sank down onto the wet earth and gulped huge lungfuls of air. The skin on his face felt brittle, hard.

It took three or four minutes to get his breath and balance back, then he hauled himself up to the pool and filled the bucket again. Back he went into the flames and smoke, and again he easily found the stump he wanted. The water seemed to douse the burning stump completely but, again, he couldn't stay to make certain.

The third trip was nearly a disaster. He found the third stump and poured the water over it but he had somehow turned himself around and he suddenly realized that he was heading down the slope, into the fire. He turned in a moment of blind panic and began to run, dropping the bucket. He ran about eight steps and collided with the hot trunk of a charred tree, falling backward onto the hot earth, gasping with the shock and pain.

His great gulp of hot air and smoke sent him choking and reeling, fear rising up inside him in a great red wave. He staggered back up the slope, blundering from side to side, a redness in front of his eyes. He tripped, nearly fell again, kept grimly fighting his way up the hill, lungs bursting.

The cold wetness of the spray from Kristian's hose hit him with a physical shock. Again he dropped to his knees and took a great gulp of air. It was better closer to the ground but it still hurt, and he choked and coughed as the smoke entered his lungs again. Kristian came through the smoke and dragged him to his feet, hauling him out over the blackened space, his hose never missing the red spots that flared around them.

"You fool, Jason! You idiot! What were you doing?"

"Thanks, buddy." He was still gulping air. "Thought I was a goner for a minute or two . . . glad you saw me . . ."

"So am I! That was stupid! What were you doing?"

"Those stumps giving off the sparks . . . think I got them, though . . . damped them down a bit, anyway . . . don't think your plastic bucket will be much use any more . . ." He tried to smile and he thought the skin on his face was cracking with the effort.

"You got 'em all right. That's how I realized

what was happening. What a stupid thing to do! The fire is passing us. In a few minutes I could have gone in there with the hose!" Even as Kristian spoke he was still playing the hose across the smoking, steaming ground. The nozzle was adjusted for a wide, soaking spray.

"See? We've got a good firebreak here now. We've driven the fire back onto ground it's already been over. As long as the trees themselves don't go up we're safe on this side. That house below us is all paved yard out the back and there isn't much stuff above us. I think we've got it beaten."

"Unless the wind brings it back, Kristian."

In the tangled gullies and ridges the wind sometimes did crazy things, swirling back and forth so that it could change direction completely in moments. Now the fire was so big that it was creating its own wind, sending unseen masses of hot air spiraling into the sky, sucking more air in at ground level. The gusts were coming solidly now, with no real pause between them, and they could not tell which blasts were the fierce northerly that had blown all day and which were caused by the fire itself. It didn't matter. Wind was wind, however it was caused.

The pool was half-empty now and Kristian turned the nozzle down to give just a narrow stream, picking out and killing the small red spots visible through the smoke.

"How is Shona doing?" Jason felt better already. His lungs were getting a little air at last and the dreadful pounding of his pulse was beginning to slow.

"I wouldn't have a clue. Been a bit busy. She's been using the hose up there, though. I can feel the pressure drop when she opens it up. She isn't wasting water, she turns it off when she isn't using it. You'd better go up there and see."

"Right. I'm gone." And he was.

Shona was feeling better. Only a few bits and pieces of burning debris had landed in her area and she'd pounced on them immediately. "I think we're winning, Jason. It never really got across the road here, and now there isn't much left over there to burn. It's dying right down."

"I think we've won, Shona. I really think we've won. You can leave this bit now. Take your hose up the other side of the house and help Kristian. He's moving onto the slope above the house."

"Is it bad on that side?"

"No, don't worry. The wind is taking it away from us. We're just playing safe."

"I like the sound of that. The word 'safe,' I mean. I haven't felt 'safe' all night!"

Kristian and Shona soon cleared the northern slope and now the fire could not approach the house at all. There was a wide area of burned grass which would offer the hungry flames no food. Kristian switched off the pump, but he remembered to pull the fuel drum out of the pool and he refilled the gas tank immediately. It might well be needed again. They sat on the edge of the veranda, resting, getting their breath and their confidence back together.

"Look at it, will you? Just look at it!" The wonder was there again in Shona's voice. "Terrible, but beautiful, too. The light, so clear . . ."

"Not beautiful at all. Ugly. Horrible." Kristian spoke with a bitterness that surprised the other two.

Yet there was a beauty to it. Where the grasses were still burning a yellow light filled the spaces between the blackened trees. It was a hard, clear light. The smoke had risen above the trees and the space underneath was a golden theater with all the lights on bright and strong. Jason, too, was struck silent by the realization that it was as Shona said it was. Beautiful. Terrible but beautiful.

"This place is safe," said Kristian. "What do we do next?"

"Well, we should probably stay here until help comes . . . I just don't know." It was the first time all night that Jason had admitted to not knowing what to do next. He had seemed to know the next move every time, and he'd become the leader of the three. Now the crisis was passing he was caught without his next move thought out.

"Well," said Kristian, "we can stay here to guard this place and wait for people to come back. We can start going around other houses to see what we can do. We can try to get up into the town. Or we can sit here all night wondering what to do next."

Shona was definite. "I want to go up to the town. I want to find out where my parents are."

"We all know what happened to my house," said Jason. "I don't want to go back down there. This place isn't in any danger now, not if we give everything a final soaking. Our people will be wondering about us."

"I don't know. I'd sort of like to stay here. Just to make sure. But you're probably right, Jason. I think this place is safe enough. And Shona's place wasn't in any real danger in the first place, nothing around it to burn. I just don't know."

"There's Mr. Robards!"

"Hello! Still here? How did you do?"

Kristian answered for all of them. His voice was a great deal more friendly than it had been when they last saw Mr. Robards. "Yes, we're still here, and so is the house. Jason is a bit scorched, though."

Robards' voice quickened with concern. "You all right?"

"Yes," said Jason. "I'm as good as gold, lost my

68

way in the smoke and got a bit hot for a few minutes but no harm done."

"Good, good. You all right, lassie?"

"Fine, sir," said Shona. "Are you all right? We wondered where you were when the main fire went through."

"Oh, I took shelter in a brick garage for a few minutes. Bit frightening, of course. What do we do now? I think the worst is well past."

"We were just talking about that, trying to make a decision."

"Well," said Mr. Robards, "I'm going to head up to the town now if I can. Have to do it on foot, though. There'll be people wondering what happened down here. Your parents, for instance."

"I think we should stick together. This place seems safe enough now but we don't know what other places are like. We'd be better off together." This was Kristian speaking, the one who'd seemed the most independent. "Just seems to make sense to stick together. And I agree that we should try to get out."

"Well, that makes it fairly clear, I suppose. We go out, and we go out together." Jason was relieved that Kristian had agreed. He didn't want them separated. They'd worked well as a team and he wanted the team to stay together.

"Well, then. We'd better go. If you're ready?"

They could tell from Mr. Robards' voice that he was trying not to give orders. Jason was glad of that; he saw himself as the leader of the team and he knew they'd done a good job. He didn't want to stop being the leader just because there was an adult about the place. At the same time, he was honest enough to admit that he felt better with Mr. Robards there.

He and Kristian gave the whole block a good wetting-down again before they left. The wind had gone, but there were still flakes of ash drifting down through the air, and there was always the possibility of a spark. There was the chance, too, that a little bark, or a twig, might still be smoldering somewhere where the water hadn't reached it. Only a few yards from the clearing the bush was still a fairyland of red and yellow light, with strings of red sparks like streamers up the sides of the trees, and dancing bonfires where fallen logs had caught. The harsh light of the flames in the gully still painted everything gold where the light hit it and black where it didn't.

As they walked along the driveway Jason turned back to look at the wallabies. They were still there, dark shapes in the shadows cast by the pool. The grass around them was still green and cool, and still wet from the hosing. The wallabies would be safe now, unless the wind came back.

Shona, Jason, and Kristian stopped for a moment at the end of the driveway. Before them lay a whole new world they had never seen before. It was their old world they were looking at but now it was a new world to them. There were houses burning in several places amongst the bush. There were smells they'd never smelled before, sounds they had never heard before. There were lights and brightnesses where the bush had always before been a somber gray-green.

There was a dull explosion somewhere amongst the trees. They'd heard the sound earlier in the night and none of them had been able to guess what it was.

"Gas tank," said Mr. Robards. "Been a few of them gone up tonight, and there'll be more before it's done with."

They started to walk up The Avenue, a dark pathway rising in a long, slow climb up the side of the ridge to the main road into the township, two or three miles away. The still-smoldering grasses and the burning bark of the trees lit the bush. The road was a dark ribbon between them, the only place where there were no spots of red light.

"Listen!" Shona had heard it first, but when she stopped them the sound came faintly to them all. "What is it?"

"It's a truck!" Kristian shouted the words. Perhaps this was his father, come to get them! "No, it's not my dad's truck. It's a small one . . . down that way?"

"There isn't any road down there," said Mr. Robards, uncertainly.

"Yes, there is," said Kristian. "Well, not exactly a road. A sort of track. It's pretty rough but sometimes I take my trailbike along it. You could get through."

The noise of the engine was quite clear now, growing louder every minute, but there was still no sign of the headlights. There was something weird about hearing the truck approach closer and closer without them being able to see anything.

"It's on The Avenue . . ." said Mr. Robards. "Coming this way . . . very slowly."

They stood still, peering down the road. How could there be a truck in that bottom end of the road? The fire had gone through there like a giant blowtorch. They all moved to the sides of the road. There was something uncanny, mysterious, almost ghostlike, about this unseen approaching truck.

It was seen first as a vague movement, then as a black shape looming in the flame-touched darkness of the road. It took shape as the dying flames reflected off the body panels, bringing shape to the dark mass. It was a Forests Commission pickup truck, moving very slowly and with no lights showing at all. When the driver saw them he slowed even more and came to a stop alongside them.

"Hello there!" The driver spoke as he climbed from the cabin. "Bit hot, eh?"

"Well, er, hello. Good evening." Mr. Robards sounded somewhat confused.

"No, mate. Not a good evening. Bit warm! That flamin' fire. That's a good one! She was flamin' all right! Nearly cooked my truck. Melted half the blasted wirin'. Lost me headlights an' everythin'. Where is everybody?"

"That's what we'd like to know," said Kristian. "There hasn't been a vehicle down here for hours."

Mr. Robards was still nonplussed. "But, er, where did you spring from? How did you get here? There wasn't anyone left down that end."

"Forests Commission, mate. I went home for me tea. Used the truck because I was only going to be gone for an hour. Fire cut me off, and I could see what was happening. Decided to come over here and lend a hand. But then it came back at another angle and cut me off again. Thought I was a goner for a few minutes! Boss won't be too happy about the truck, either. I wasn't really supposed to borrow it, you might say."

"Well, we're glad you did. And I'm sure your boss won't mind, under the circumstances. What news is there? And how the devil did you get in here?" It wasn't like Mr. Robards to speak so quickly, Shona thought.

"Came in over the ridge. Old track through there. Bit rough, but she's a four-wheel drive. News? Well, that's all a bit confused. Fires everywhere. They said on the radio that hundreds of houses are gone, but then the heat got the radio. Don't know too much at the moment. Can't we get on up to the town? That's where I thought I'd better go."

"I don't think you can get out yet. This is the only road and things still look a little warm up there." Jason pointed at the outline of the ridge that led into the town. There was still a huge red glow lighting up the underside of the smoke banks up there. There was obviously still a major fire going up toward the town.

"Well, I might give it a try, anyway. Want a lift? She'll be a bit slow without the lights, but at least we can see the road."

"Er, thank you, yes, we would. We'd all be better off on the truck, I think." The children agreed and they climbed into the back. Mr. Robards went around to the passenger door and climbed into the cabin. The driver slid behind the wheel and started the engine, but then he climbed out again.

"Look, kids. It's still pretty hot, right? Could be more fires blowin' through. Still plenty left to burn. Stay down low, all right? If it gets too hot, the sides will give you some protection. Fair enough?"

They nodded and he climbed back into the cab.

The truck began to wind its slow way up the slope. From the back, the children could see further and as the truck climbed slowly higher an even wider view of the disaster opened up before them.

No one spoke. There was nothing to say. They sat still, staring, each with his or her own thoughts. The truck ground slowly forward, at less than a walking pace. Everyone on the truck knew that they were still a long way and a long time from safety. They didn't even know that they were headed for a safe area, but The Avenue was the only way out in any case, so there was no choice. There hadn't been many choices available at any time through that long evening.

"There's someone down there! There's someone walking in the trees!" Jason was standing, pointing into the bush to their left.

The truck stopped and in a moment the shadowy figure came up out of the trees, across the charred and smoking grass. The smoke was almost gone and they could clearly see the man as he hurried up the slope. He walked quite casually up to the driver's door.

"It's Curly Baxter, a friend of Dad's," said Jason.

"Well, hello young Jason. Nice to see someone else! Bit hot, eh?" He was trying to sound calm but they could all hear the shake in his voice.

"Where did you come from, mate?" The driver

was surprised. They were all surprised. For hours they had been alone, behind the front of the fire, knowing that no one could get through to them, yet here was Curly Baxter. He must have been alone through the worst of it. Jason realized that, like them, Curly had thought he was alone. How many others might there be?

Curly swung up over the back wheel and climbed onto the truck. "Bit hairy, isn't it? Thanks for the lift. Didn't fancy walking out through this lot!" He sat down with his back against the cabin wall, and a white grin broke through his blackened face. Jason thought he was either trying to keep them from being frightened or he was trying to keep down the fear in himself.

The fear began to slide away from Jason. The fire was past them, up the hill, toward the town, along the ridge. The road went up the side of the slope and onto that ridge, but at the speed the fire had been moving the worst of it must be well past. They'd all be safe now.

The air was not as hot as it had been and they could all breathe easily. The grass was all gone from under the trees and night had brought blackness to the sky behind them. The trees still burning gave the driver enough light to see the road.

"What's in these drums?" Curly tapped one with his knuckles. "They're full. Is it water?"

"I don't know," said Jason. "I'll ask the driver."

"No need. Hang on a minute." With hands that had worked hard for years, Curly had no trouble loosening the cap of one drum. "Gas! I'll be . . . gasoline! Hey! Hey!" He was banging on the roof of the cabin with his fists. The truck stopped with a jolt that sent them all sliding forward in the back.

"What's the problem?" It was the driver, stepping down from the cabin.

"Problem? You idiot! Problem? Just a couple of drums of fuel out here in the open with us, you clown! Gasoline! And there just happens to be a small bushfire going on at the moment. You've got us riding beside a bomb, mate." That was the longest speech Curly had ever made. Jason had never seen him excited before, let alone angry, but he was very definitely excited now, and angry.

"Get rid of it, you fool!"

"Fair go, mate. Settle down a bit. I didn't know how far I'd have to go. I came in through the bush, remember? I need spare fuel."

"Yes, yes, I know all about that! But not out here with us and the fire! Put it in the cabin with you!"

"In the cabin? You must be joking!"

"Makes sense. Think about it. Out here it is in the heat. Any leak or fumes, then just one spark . . . put it in the cabin. Or dump it. And you can't dump it, so wake up. Get yourself into gear!"

Mr. Robards cut in. "Well, there is an alternative. I don't want to share the back of this truck with drums of gas either, but your fuel tanks must have room now for some of the stuff in the drums. Why not top up your tanks?"

"Yes, I could do that. If we found a safe spot. Be a bit exciting if she caught fire while we were pouring fuel all over the place!" The driver grinned whitely in the darkness.

In the end, Curly made the necessary decisions. He took a piece of hose from a deserted house and siphoned the fuel into the tanks. "Now, keep your hands around the hose where it goes into the tank. Don't leave any gaps. Seal it up tight. Jason, you cover the opening into the drum. Put your hands around the hose like this. Don't leave room for even a single spark." Within a few minutes the drums were empty. The fuel was in the safety of the tanks.

"What about the drums, Mr. Baxter?" Kristian asked. "We could fill them with water from a swimming pool or something. It might be handy."

"Yes, good idea. At least we could wet ourselves down if necessary."

That was fairly hard to do. There were swimming pools at nearly every house, but the drums were difficult to push down into the water, and when they were full they were hard to carry. Still, it was managed, and now the truck had a small water supply. Curly had insisted that the drums be stuffed into the cabin. The driver wasn't happy about it but he could see the point Curly was making.

"We've got to be able to lie flat out here. Get some protection from the sides of the truck, see. That means giving ourselves plenty of room. Course, it'd be better if we could all shelter in the cab, but we can't. No real choice, see?"

CHAPTER 15

The truck was crawling back up the slope now, slower than a walking man, slower, Kristian thought, than a dead-tired, staggering man; he wondered where that thought had come from. The road was a ribbon of darker blackness among the trees and grass, picked out between the glows of smaller fires where stumps and posts still burned, or where logs smoldered. Small patches of dried grass sometimes flared into light and were instantly consumed by the fierce little flames. The earlier fire had taken all the moisture from them. There were no leaves on the small trees now and where they could be seen in silhouette against some blaze further back in the bush they seemed distorted, twisted by the heat.

The road had a concrete curb and the driver was managing to keep his darkened truck on the pavement but it was a slow process. So far they had covered only about a mile.

"What if it comes again?" Shona thought, and she realized that she'd spoken aloud when Curly Baxter put his arm around her shoulders. "We've finished with it now, young Shona. It won't be back. There isn't much left to burn!"

They were nearly up to the main road when they came to the first burning houses. There were no other people in the world around them and it was appalling to watch one, two, a dozen houses burning fiercely, well beyond saving. The houses were all set a long way back from the road but the heat they gave off came almost solidly across the road. They were forced to turn their heads and then to kneel down on the bed of the truck. The air was so dry again that once more it hurt to breathe.

"Allens' place is gone." Jason's voice sounded utterly calm. None of them could really believe what they were seeing. "That's Bowens' . . . look, even the garage is collapsing. Look!" As Shona raised her eyes the roof of the garage collapsed and a hot blast swept over the truck like the breath of some giant dragon.

"There's one we can save!" It was one of the men, and as the truck stopped he was already swinging down onto the black road. The three men were running across the charred grass to a house which was still undamaged and the three children followed them.

"Hey! Back to the truck, kids! You'll be safer there."

"That might be true," thought Kristian, "but it doesn't matter. I'm having a crack at this fire." The fear in him had given way to anger. Now he wanted to fight the fire, to crush it, destroy it. He wanted to hit back and to hit back hard. So far they had only been defending themselves. Now it was time to attack.

The wooden decking at the back of the house was alight but the flames had not caught any part of the house itself. The men began to pull at the decking, rocking and swaying it on its tall posts. The rocking and swaying grew and Shona suddenly felt that the movement was in her head and that she was losing her balance. She fought the moment down, forced the nausea back. She knew that there must be tanks of water here somewhere! Where? Where? She ran around the side of the house, passing from light into blackness so intense that she could see nothing. Kristian and Jason were suddenly with her and her night vision slowly came back.

"Jason! A hose! Where's the tap?" She grabbed the end of the hose and turned to where the fire nibbled at the posts of the decking.

"There isn't any power! You'll only get a dribble!" But he'd opened the tap on the tank and she felt the water begin to flow. He was right about the pressure but a dribble of water was better than no water at all and she edged closer to the flames, holding the hose ahead of her so the dribbling stream fell on the seats of the flames.

With a great moaning and groaning the decking pulled free of the house and crashed out onto what had once been a garden. Once, long ago, or only an hour or two ago? The men were using pieces of wood to scratch and scrabble at the decking timber, slowly moving it further from the house. Shona dragged her limp hose around, dribbling water on the small fires which still tried to eat their way into the collapsed woodwork.

Suddenly it was over. The fires were out. The men and the two boys were stamping out small spots which still smoldered but there was no fire on any part of the house. Shona stood still, letting the water flow away through the ashes. Had they saved the house? Had they managed to fight back?

"We did it, Shona! We saved one! One less house for this thing to eat up. One blow for us! We won! We'll beat this fire! We'll kill it! We'll beat it all! Just you wait and see!" Kristian was talking so quickly his words were falling over each other. He was almost shouting and she knew that some sort of reaction was taking hold of him. They were all becoming emotional and she knew that that was still dangerous.

She took him by the arm. "Kristian, slow down. Take it easy. It isn't all over yet, and we have to stay calm. We have to be careful." She kept her voice very calm and steady.

"You kids all right? No one scorched?" It was Curly Baxter. It was like him to worry about everyone else. He wasn't a young man, and his clothes were singed and burned in a dozen places. "OK, back to the truck. We might save a few more."

"Lots more," thought Kristian. His anger had given way to a quiet determination. "There must be other houses like that one, houses we can save. It's a way of hitting back, and I want to do that."

On the truck they looked back at the house. There were still ashes smoldering and the stumps of the posts were still glowing, but there was a black band around the house where no sparks could be seen. The ruined decking was burning itself out, well away from the house.

"Could use a pump or two, eh?" The driver of the truck was wearing his Forests Commission uniform and this seemed to give him some authority, or perhaps it was just that he'd brought the truck and the truck had brought them all together as a team. If the team had a leader, the driver would be the one.

"We haven't really got a leader," thought Jason. "We just worked as a team without anyone giving any orders, and we saved that house. We saved it. Three men and three kids. With no tools. With hardly any water."

"An axe or two, or even a crowbar, would help."

"A few cold cans would help, too!" There was a brief laugh. The men were joking about the fire. Perhaps they had no other way to talk about it. Shona just felt weary. What did one house matter when so many were burning?

"Where do we go now?" she asked the driver. "Can we get through to the town yet?"

"I don't know, love. I wouldn't like to try it. Look at the color of the sky up that way."

There was an angry red glow rising above the trees along the top of the ridge. Shona knew that there were houses all along both sides of the road up there and she had a sudden, frightening picture of what was happening. The road along that ridge held many of the town's older houses, some of them grand old homes that had been there for more than a century. The gardens held huge trees, far older than the people who enjoyed their shade. It was a beautiful road, green and shaded, with views of the distant hills showing blue through the green of the trees. Or it had been beautiful before all this happened.

Curly said that he thought they'd be of more use

if they stayed in The Avenue and tried to save whatever houses they could. "We can do a fair bit of good right here. I don't think we could get up to the town just yet, and there'll be all sorts of people up there to fight the fire by now. We'd just be in the way."

"Well, we can't do much with the kids here. I think we should try to get them out first." This was the driver, his voice coming from the darkness where he squatted against the rear wheels of the truck.

"I don't know so much about that," said Curly. "I saw six people fighting to save that house, not three adults and three children; six people. And as far as I'm concerned they were all doing a good job."

"Yes, I know that. I'm not knocking their help, but they are only kids . . ."

"We aren't just 'kids,'" said Kristian. "We're people who live in this place. We have a right to stay here and fight. And we want to do just that."

Jason supported him. "This is our home. We've already done some good. We've saved two houses now. We can save more. We want to try, anyway."

"OK, OK," said the driver. "I suppose I agree with you, really. I just want to do the right thing."

"We can't get out yet, anyway." Mr. Robards' voice came as a surprise. He didn't say much and, perhaps because of that, people tended to listen to what he had to say. "If we can't get out, we have to stay. And if we have to stay we might as well fight the fire. All of us."

This ended all suggestion of trying to get up to the main township area. "We'll go up to the top of this road and we'll see what we can work out. We'll be able to see more from up there than we can down here." The driver climbed into the cabin and started the motor. No other words were spoken.

The truck began to climb the slope again, following the black pathway that was the road. Even without headlights it was easy to see where the roadway led. Small tufts of grass were still burning and the blackened trees still wore ribbons of glowing bark. There were no leaves.

The glow reflected off the low banks of smoke overhead, lighting their great ridges and valleys in a terrifying range of unnatural reds, yellows and oranges. Shona thought again what a beautiful sight it was and then felt surprise that she could see any beauty in such a dreadful scene. Yet she couldn't keep the feeling away. There was a beauty in it all, a wild, savage beauty, but a genuine one for all that. She knew that she would remember this night as long as she lived and she knew, too, that she would never be able to describe it to anyone else well enough to have them see it as she was seeing it now. She consciously tried to preserve all the details in her mind.

At the first intersection the driver turned left. This road led back down to the valley, but the truck stopped. Those on the back of the truck looked forward over the cab, and they caught their breath at the sight that lay before them. None had ever seen anything like it.

They were facing the side of another great ridge, running parallel to the one they were climbing. This was normally a green wall over which the tops of the far mountains could be seen in a blue and misty outline. The ridge was usually a mass of greens in every shade, with areas of gray eucalyptus and the brighter colors of imported trees adding variation to the colors. In the spring the walls of the ridge were a tapestry of life, framing the valley below, but now they were a tapestry of destruction.

The ridge seemed to hang over the valley like a great, black curtain. Everywhere along it there were red spots where trees were burning. With the ridge so black and the sky so dark that they could barely be told apart, the red spots seemed to be hanging in the sky like an evil constellation, like angry, red clouds of stars. There were seven, eight, no, nine large orange balls of light, hanging among the red.

"Houses."

There was a silence. "Fourteen houses."

"That's it, then. There were only a few houses over there. If they've all gone they must have had it hot and fast up there."

Another silence. This time the silence lasted long enough for them all to hear the movement of the wind again, and the distant roar of the fire still going ahead, still devouring the bush and the houses. "Strange," thought Jason, "I haven't noticed the sound of the fire for a long time, now. Yet it was the sound of it that scared me most of all when it first came through."

"Let's see whether we can do any good down here," the driver called back from his window.

They were in a darker area now, one where the fire had flown overhead or passed around the houses and the gardens, and the first four homes they passed were not touched. They seemed strangely lifeless, just darkened blocks against the night sky, with no noise and no light and no life at all. The fifth house was ablaze.

There was nothing that could be done. Kristian wanted to see whether anything could be saved but Mr. Robards told him quite calmly that there was nothing they could do. Houses that had fire inside them were a job for experts with the proper equipment. "All we can do, laddie, is help where the fire has not really caught. Once the house is alight, there's nothing we can do. It's gone, I'm afraid."

The burning house gave more light here and the driver accelerated a little, though this road was narrower than The Avenue. Again he called back from the cabin. "Are there any more houses down here? This looks like a dead end."

Mr. Robards looked at Jason. "Any more houses down here, Jason?"

"Yes. There's Pipers' place. Another white brick house, and then Allens'."

"It might be best if we don't think about the names, laddie. Names mean people. Let's just think of them as fires we have to stop." He leaned over the edge of the cabin roof and spoke to the driver. The truck moved forward again with a jolt that nearly threw Kristian over the side. He'd been standing, staring silently at the fire inside the house.

At first there had been just a dull glow through the windows, almost as if someone had left a light showing inside. Then the light had begun to brighten and to take on a stronger, red color. Furniture could be seen as outlines against the growing light. Suddenly the flames had blossomed outward through the windows and under the roof, pouring thick smoke into the air and rapidly eating through every opening and every gap. The whole house was suddenly ablaze where only a moment earlier there had been just that dull glow from the windows.

As the truck moved away the flames found their

way through the roof and the house became an orange fireball. Kristian could not believe that a whole house could be consumed so quickly and he could not believe that it could generate such a fierce heat. The skin on his face felt dry and brittle again; he ran his hand up and down one cheek, still staring at the bonfire that had been a house. The jolting of the truck brought him back to full awareness. There would be other houses. Kristian promised himself that they'd save some of them.

CHAPTER 16

Kristian was right. The group kept the promise he'd made to himself. They saved at least one more house and probably several others. Four times they jumped from the truck to run across to houses where deckings and verandas, posts and retaining walls were beginning to burn. They were realizing that many houses were burned after the main rush of the fire and not at its height. With no tools, the work was both backbreaking and heartbreaking. There was nothing they could do but pull away everything that was starting to burn, and throw it back, well clear.

The three adults were quite definite about not trying to save any house that had already had fire inside it. That was too dangerous. It would also waste time. Without water they couldn't save a house that was already alight. They would only risk injury and they would be wasting time that could better be spent on houses where there was a chance of success.

They did save one house that had begun to burn. It was a long, narrow house of cement sheeting. They were almost past it when Kristian saw the tell-tale red glow underneath. He thumped on the roof and the truck stopped.

There was a garage underneath the back of the house and the glow was coming from a burning trailer and a pile of firewood, both under the garage roof. All six of them went to work without any instructions from anyone. There was a tap on a small tank at the end of the house and Shona found a tin bucket she could fill, though it was a slow business. The men hauled the trailer clear and left it to burn. Jason and Kristian began throwing the firewood clear, kicking the burning pieces away with their boots. It was hot and heavy work but within ten minutes everything that had caught fire was well clear of the house.

"That wasn't a bad job. Well done, everyone." Mr. Robards gave Kristian a pat on the shoulder as he spoke.

"Too right," the driver agreed. "She'd have well and truly gone up in another few minutes. We can call that a win. One more we've saved."

"Hey! Look at that! We haven't saved it yet!" Curly was pointing at the bottom of the back wall. There was a dull glow showing cherry-red through the cement sheeting at the bottom of the wall. "Water, Shona! Fill that bucket!"

Kristian knew what had happened. In any timber-framed house there are soleplates running along the bottom of the wall, long pieces of timber on which the wall is built. Over the years cobwebs, sawdust and even leaves will collect in the bottom of the wall cavity, on the soleplates. Somehow a spark had got inside the wall and set fire to that rubbish.

He kicked a hole in the wall, aware of a certain excitement at the thought of simply kicking a hole in a wall. Shona ran up with her bucket and poured the water, quite carefully, all along the opening. The hole was two yards long and it took the whole bucketful, but that was enough to put it out. The men had filled their hard hats with water, too, and now they went right along the wall, knocking holes through the sheeting and dribbling the water onto the soleplates. It took only a few minutes for the glow to disappear. Now the house was safe.

"Well done, both of you. She's right, now." Curly grinned.

They went right around the house but there were no more signs of any fire in the house itself. The fence was burning but they couldn't do anything much about that.

As they walked back to the truck Jason spoke to Kristian. "Another house on the list of survivors

. . . You're getting your wish. We are hitting back."
He'd spoken very quietly and then walked on. Kristian stood looking after him for a moment. Was it that obvious? Did they all know how he felt about this red monster they were fighting? Did they, perhaps, all feel the same way?

Back on the truck they began once more the long, slow climb out of the valley and up to the town. They came out of the bushland where the road turned for the straight run up the shoulder of the ridge. At the top there was a sharp turn onto the main western road into the town. Though it was the main western entrance it was really just a single lane of pavement with badly broken edges. It connected the town only with the new subdivisions in the gullies around The Avenue. For all the people in these new areas, the ridge road was the only way out into the world of work, of marketplaces and shopping centers, of playing fields and pony clubs. It was the lifeline for all those new subdivisions, the only lifeline.

Now that lifeline was choked.

The truck pushed past two burned-out cars lying side by side, one of them in the middle of the road. They were almost afraid to look inside the cars as they passed, but they did so. There was no one inside.

Up the slope they climbed, into the growing heat where the fire was still very active. The ridge road had led through a beautiful area that was now a ruin, a lost world of destruction. All the graceful old houses were gone. All the trees in the formal gardens were burning. Down in The Avenue the trees had been scorched and the leaves had been swept from them, but up here the fire had been much hotter and the trunks themselves were burning.

A giant old pine tree was burning on the corner, a huge candle of pure energy. The whole tree seemed white, the center of a giant pillar of clear, pulsating energy. The flames were suspended in the air, dancing and wavering well out from the tree itself, feeding on the energy given off, consuming the tree without seeming to touch it. High overhead there was a cone of flame standing up into the night sky over the top of the tree. The waves of heat were painful even a hundred and fifty yards away.

The driver stopped the truck. "We aren't going past that just yet. We'll wait till it dies down. It'd cook us!"

And so they waited. For half an hour they waited, watching spellbound as the tree was eaten away by flames that never seemed to actually touch it. Slowly the heat began to lessen and the flames in the air seemed to close in on the tree. They settled on it and began to finish the work of consuming it completely. The little group watched in grim fascination. Somehow this was worse than seeing a house burn. That tree had taken perhaps a century to grow, or even more. It was a landmark. Yet, in less than an hour it had been eaten up. Devoured. Consumed. Gone forever. It was a tragic sight. The houses were artificial things and could be replaced but that tree was, had been, part of mother nature, part of the earth itself, for longer than anyone could remember. This was nature devouring itself.

When the heat fell away enough they continued their slow haul to safety. They turned the corner and made their way along the ridge road. No one spoke. There was nothing to say. This was a holocaust. Everything was gone.

The great homes were piles of brick and ash with flames dancing over them, seeking out any last pieces of fuel, consuming everything that could burn. House after house after house, all were gone.

Heat washed over the silent watchers on the slowly moving truck. It was a sharp, hurtful heat but they ignored it. Not one of them could really believe what they were seeing. Even after the flames were gone they would have trouble accepting the vast proof of this disaster.

They saw things so far beyond belief that later they would not be able to trust even their own memories. They saw the remains of a boat and a boat-trailer laid out on the ground in outlines of melted aluminum, only the motor still a solid object and even that was half melted. They saw steel gates twisted into shapes that no one could have imagined. They saw flames on the piles of rubble in colors no one would ever believe. They saw light with a savage purity and they felt heat as they had never felt it before nor would ever feel it again.

They put it all behind them. They were close to the town now, close to where safety lay, to where safety must lie, had to lie, or all was lost. The truck crept forward, twisting and turning past abandoned and burned-out cars, boats, caravans, and the charred body of a cow.

None of them saw the horse at first in the darkness and the smoke. The sound of hooves on the asphalt road made them aware. It wasn't loud and there was still a distant roaring from the wind and the fire, but this was a rhythmic sound. It was somehow a sad, lost and lonely sound. Shona heard it first, perhaps because she'd heard it so many times before. She looked back behind the truck, peering into the swirling smoke, and so she saw it before the others.

It was moving slowly and the gait was uneven. Shona knew at once that this animal, too, had suffered in the last few violent hours. She tried to stand but the heat was intense and she could feel it sharp and hot upon her hair and her face. She called to the men but no one heard her. Keeping down on the floor she crawled forward again. It seemed to take ages to attract attention but when she caught the arm of Mr. Robards and pointed back behind the truck he turned and saw the horse at once.

He thumped on the roof of the truck. Nothing happened. He thumped again, harder. The noise was still too strong for the driver to hear him. He leaned over the side and called through the window. Shona couldn't hear the words but she knew the truck was not going to stop.

"Make him stop! Make him stop!" She was screaming, trying to make them all understand. Dimly she heard the driver call back something about the heat.

"Mr. Robards, that horse is hurt! We've got to help it!"

"We can't, girlie. We can't do anything for it." Even with all the noise in the air, even with the sky itself cracking open with the heat, she could hear the sadness in his voice. "He'll have to take his chances! There's nothing we can do!"

Shona didn't argue. She knew there wasn't anything they could do. They were still in danger themselves. She crawled back to the rear of the truck and leaned out as far as she could.

"Here, boy! Come on! Catch up, boy, please!

Please catch up! Follow us. Come on, boy. We're going where it's safe. Come on, come on, follow us."

Perhaps it could hear her voice. Perhaps it was just following blindly. She heard the hooves break into a canter and the horse came up to the truck. She could almost touch it and she reached out her arm. Stronger arms caught her from behind and she was dragged back into the truck. It was Mr. Robards and he bent down over her. "Stay in the truck, girlie! It's a bit hot to go looking for someone who might fall out! The horse will be all right, now. It'll follow us out."

She could never work out afterwards just how long it took them to get back to the township itself but she could always remember the clop-clop-clop of the horse's hooves on the pavement as it followed them up the road. It was a lonely sound. She caught glimpses of the horse whenever the smoke shifted. It was only a few feet behind the truck all the way.

"It trusts us," she thought. "It knows we'll lead it out of all this. Even with all this going on around it, it thinks that we'll get it out."

"Poor animal," Mr. Robards was thinking. "Badly burned on the withers. Probably have to be put down if it does get out. There should be more we can do, but these children have to be got out first."

And still they could hear the steady clop, clop, clop behind them. The truck was moving slowly and the horse was staying right behind it. Shona began to believe that they'd save the horse after all. It couldn't be far to the town now and there would be fire trucks there, fire fighters, safety. It was only then that Shona began to feel afraid again. There hadn't been time for much fear once the fire had arrived. She curled up as flat on the floor as possible seeking the shelter of the low steel sides of the truck.

Later, much later, she was to wonder what happened to the horse. It wasn't behind them when they reached the town.

CHAPTER 17

The driver was becoming even more worried.
There was still no sign of the fire crews who must
be up here somewhere. There was no sign of any
living thing at all. They were alone in a crazy world
of heat, an insane world of flame, a violent, vicious,
sad world of destruction. Black shadows danced in
the darkness. Red gouts of flame would suddenly
shoot into the sky and then fall back again. Crawling, snaking lines of fire ran along the ground.
Outlines shimmered and moved. Details blurred
and twisted. Movements were imagined.

"There's someone over there!" Shona had seen
a movement through the smoke and the glare. It
was hard to be certain with the shadows and the
sudden bursts of light seeming to make everything
shift and dance before her eyes, but she thought
she'd seen a person moving in the light from a

burning house. Just a dimly seen movement seen in silhouette, perhaps nothing at all, but . . .

"Here! Quick!" Curly was banging on the cabin, the signal for a stop.

"Over . . . there. I . . . think it is someone. I'm not . . . not sure . . ."

Everyone stood still, suffering the heat on their faces. Through streaming, smoke-stung eyes they searched the burning piles of rubble and the darker gaps between the burned bushes and trees. There was nothing. Once Jason thought he saw a movement but a rolling bank of smoke blocked his view and he had to cover his eyes.

"There he is!" It was Shona who saw him again. Her eyes seemed to cope with the stinging smoke better than anyone else's eyes could. "He's seen us! Over here! Over here!" Everyone began shouting and the driver pushed the horn button down hard and held it there.

They were heard. A blackened figure staggered out of the smoke bank and fell on the road on hands and knees. The three teenagers ran across the road as the men brought the truck back. They helped the scarecrow figure to its feet.

"It's all right. We've got you. You're safe now." Shona was talking softly, reassuring, calming. The smoke-blackened figure was that of a young girl about twelve years old. None of them knew her.

At first she couldn't speak. They helped her up onto the truck. She immediately slipped down on the floor and lay there, staring into the boiling, rolling sky. The men looked at her and then at each other.

"We've got to get out quickly. That kid needs help." There was urgency in Mr. Robards' voice.

"Well, I can follow the road well enough," said the driver. "I can see it well enough. The problem is the heat . . ."

"We'll all keep down on the floor. The sides will give us enough protection. We can't get into the cabin, and we can't stay here." Jason was working out all the angles. "This girl will have to lie down anyway, so she'll have to stay on the back."

"Come on, man! Let's move!" Mr. Robards was speaking to the driver, who still stood on the road, looking ahead.

"It isn't that easy . . . what if there are power lines down, across the road? Even a fallen tree, if we hit it . . . I don't like this at all."

"For heaven's sake, man, none of us like it! But what choice do we have? This kid needs medical help. Right now!"

"Yes, yes, I know all that . . . well, all right. Keep your fingers crossed!"

He swung up into the cabin and the truck bounced forward, moving faster now as the driver desperately swung the wheel from side to side. He was bent over the wheel, peering forward through the sooty glass, trying to see in the swirling twists of light. It was slow, frustrating work. Curly Baxter was becoming agitated.

"This kid isn't breathing too well, you know, Robards. She's getting air, but she's unconscious, or just about. I don't like the look of her at all."

"Not much more we can do, Curly. All we can do is get her out. And we can't do that any faster than we are. Keep checking her. Can you handle mouth-to-mouth resuscitation?"

"Yes, I can, but she's got a few burns, too. Shock. It's shock that kills people, you know. I reckon she's in a fair bit of pain . . ." Old Curly put a feedbag from the truck over the girl's legs. "Not much need to keep her warm here, at any rate. We're all warm enough. Here you go, lassie . . . you'll be fine, you'll see. Just keep breathing steadily . . . that's it. Won't be long, now." He remained bent over the child, talking softly, ignoring the heat washing over the truck and beating down on his back.

Kristian tried to imagine the truck as it must have seemed to anyone who could stand back and watch it. There were now seven people on the vehicle, all of them singed and blackened. All of them with clothes torn and ripped. All of them with red, weeping eyes. "What a ragged lot we must look," he thought. "Not a hose or a tank of water between us. No first-aid kit. What are we doing here? Why are we doing this?"

Jason looked again at Kristian and again he knew what Kristian was thinking. He shouted, "We're doing well, pal. Nearly out now. Three houses saved. A rescue. It isn't much when you look around you, but at least we struck a blow, eh?"

"Yes, you're right. A blow. One blow. But have a look around. The fire is just eating up the whole town. There's nothing left!"

"True. But we have done a bit. A little bit, but better than nothing!"

"Jason, I'm starting to really hate this fire. I'm not frightened anymore. I just hate it now. I'm angry. I want to fight it. I want to kill it. I want to smash it and smash it and smash it . . ."

"I know, I know. But there'll be help soon. When we get into the town . . . then we can fight back!"

"Yes . . . no . . . maybe. I don't know whether this thing can ever be stopped."

"It will be, buddy. You know that. No fire can go on forever. Just stay cool."

"That's a good one, Jason. Stay cool! Even the air is so hot it feels like breathing broken glass!"

"Well, I wouldn't know. I haven't breathed any air for an hour or so, just smoke. We're just breathing smoke." And the two boys grinned at each other, their teeth showing white in black faces,

faces streaked by tears running from their watering eyes.

Curly Baxter was still bent over the stranger, his fingers on the girl's pulse. He didn't look very happy.

CHAPTER 18

With everyone lying as flat as they could on the floor the truck ran the gauntlet of the flames, twisting and turning as sudden flares of light showed the driver the bends of the road and the obstacles that lay on or across it. The heat grew even greater, more terrible, unbearable, and then they were through. The heat fell away and they raised their faces from the floor.

It had been only a hundred yards through the worst of it.

There were fire fighters, police, people everywhere. There was a great tangle of trucks parked at crazy angles on the banks of the road. There was noise and there was action. There was water! Trucks lined up along the middle of the road were pouring huge streams of water onto the flames, and the air they drove through now was cold. The physical shock of the sudden coolness took their breath away.

No one noticed them. Everyone they could see was busy with hoses or with pumps, with vehicles or with beaters and scrapers, with knapsack sprays. The fire fighters were blackened and grimy, lines down their faces where tears had run from their stinging eyes and through the soot on their cheeks.

The driver kept going, on toward the crossroads that marked the center of the town, moving more slowly again, bumping over hoses hard with the pressure of the water in them, braking suddenly as people ran in front of him, moving forward between the fire trucks whenever the way opened up for him.

At the crossroads they were stopped. Four police cars blocked the intersection but for a narrow gap. Still no one said anything. This was safety. This was what they'd longed for and what they'd almost stopped believing in. This was where they had been trying for hours to reach but it was not the town they had known. It was not the town the children had come through on their way home from school only a few hours earlier.

The town was forever changed. The church was gone. The service station was gone. Two shops near the corner were smoldering piles of twisted iron sheets. The fire had hit the very center of the town.

"Where are you going, driver?" There was a policeman at the driver's door. The moment passed and they simply accepted the sights they were seeing. "Where have you come from?"

The driver grinned. "I went home for me tea. Now I'm going back to work. Why? D'you want a lift somewhere?"

The policeman stared at him, but Mr. Robards leaned forward from the back of the truck. His voice showed the alarm he felt. "Officer, we've got a girl here we found along the road. She's not too well. Is there a doctor, or an ambulance?"

The policeman looked into the back of the truck. "Stay right here. We'll have someone for you in a moment. Pull to the side, driver." He began to speak into the radio he was carrying.

The driver reversed his truck onto the grassy bank in front of the ruined church. Before they were all off the truck, an ambulance was pulling in beside them. The red roof-light was throwing a dancing beam across the scene, almost like another fire. The ambulance attendants lifted the girl gently onto a stretcher and slid it swiftly into the back of their vehicle.

"Will she be all right?" Shona caught the sleeve of the ambulance driver.

"I think so, miss. Looks like she's a bit shocked and she's breathed a bit too much smoke. We'll give her some oxygen and I think she'll be fine in a day or two." He swung into his seat. The ambulance backed around onto the road, wound between the police cars and was gone into the darkness, down the road to the highway, the siren swiftly fading into the background noise.

"Now, what are we going to do with you lot? How many of you are there? Five. Best give me your names. People will be worried about you." The policeman already had a notebook in his hands.

Mr. Robards spoke. "There were six of us, seven if you count the young lass in the ambulance. Curly Baxter was with us a moment ago . . . He'll have gone to help on a fire truck. He's all right. This chap is a driver from the Forests Commission. He came over to help hours ago and got caught behind the fire. It's these children . . . their parents won't know what's happened . . ."

"Very good, sir. I won't worry about your names just now. Get into that car over there and we'll send you down to the evacuation center. You'll find everyone there, I'm sure. What about you, driver?"

"Well, mate, I came over to see if I could help. I'm fine. Don't need any evacuation center. Just want a job to do. Fought a few fires in me time, I have."

"Right, take your truck up to the recreation reserve — you know where that is? Good. There's a report center there. They'll tell you where you can be useful. Now shift your truck. It's a bit crowded round here!"

"Fair enough." He started the motor. "How bad is it, mate?"

"Very bad. The worst it could be. And it isn't over yet. We still don't have the full picture. Now, shift that truck. And listen, you did a good job with that lot. Thanks for bringing the kids out, OK?"

"No sweat, mate. All in a day's work for the forestry men!" And then he, too, was gone.

"Now, sir, if you and the kids will get in that car we'll send you down the hill."

"Certainly, officer, but I think I could be more useful up here."

"Look, sir, we've got all the men we need up here. You take these kids out and help them find their people. That's the best thing you could do. Come on, now."

Within a few moments the three teenagers and Mr. Robards were in a patrol car, leaving the stricken town behind them. At any other time it would have been a thrilling ride. The driver had his siren going and the blue roof-light flashed a pattern on the banks and cuttings of the mountain road. They should have found it exciting. There was a stream of water tankers and fire engines winding up the hill in the opposite direction, moving in to join the fight. There were red lights flashing, blue lights flashing, yellow lights flashing.

There were horns, and sirens. They were riding in a patrol car, but all the children could feel was an overwhelming tiredness, a weariness that was deep in their bones and deep in their minds. None of them spoke.

113

CHAPTER 19

The evacuation center was set up on the new sportsground at Kapana. There were hundreds of cars and trucks along the roads. The oval was covered with cars and with the odd caravan or boat rescued from the fires. Trucks were unloading cartons and boxes. One truck held a huge load of gray blankets. There were Salvation Army and Red Cross vans where people were getting sandwiches and cups of soup. It was an amazing sight but the three children didn't take it in. They were looking for particular faces.

The policeman was talking quietly to Mr. Robards. "Stay with them until you can hand them over. Their people should be here somewhere, but it might take a while to find them. It's a mess. There are desks on the right as you go in. Report there. Got all that? Good. I'd better get back."

The car turned and accelerated back out onto the road.

"Well, here we are. Everyone still all right?" They assured him they were but they weren't really listening to him. They were scanning the crowd, looking for faces. "Er, we have to report in, but first, well, I wanted to tell you how proud . . . you've all done a great job, er . . . I'm proud . . . We'd better report in. Come along."

Kristian never made it to the desks. His father came running out of the darkness and gathered him up in his great arms. "Kris! Thank God! Thank God! Your mother . . . come on, boy! Your mother, she's been so afraid. You're all right? Sure? Quick, come to your mother!"

There was no chance to say good-bye. Kristian was gone but the others barely noticed. Mr. Robards was at the desk, giving their names. Shona and Jason were still looking around but they couldn't find their parents anywhere. The whole vast building was full of people moving around. There were people with scorched clothes, people with bandages, people still wearing swimsuits and even underwear. There were people with tears on their faces, and some people standing quite still, saying nothing.

The woman at the desk was checking her lists. "Shona Anderson. Anderson, Anderson, let me see . . . yes, here we are! Your parents are here, Shona. Are you all right? There is food here, and something to drink. Do you want a doctor? No?

115

Sure? Wait a minute." She picked up a microphone and her voice went out over the amplifiers. "We have Shona Anderson at the desk. Shona Anderson." Shona felt suddenly shy, standing there in her scorched and blackened clothes, with so many people turning to look at her.

She saw two faces that drove all the shyness from her mind. The shyness, the weariness, the fear, all disappeared as she ran toward her parents. They embraced her together in a great mass of arms and bodies. Mr. Robards was watching them with a great smile on his face.

"Jason Shortland . . . let me see, Shortland. My goodness, these lists are a mess. Shortland! Here we are, Jason. Your father is here. Before I call him, do you need anything?"

Jason shook his head. All he needed at this moment were his parents but he couldn't speak. There was a great lump in his throat and suddenly he was very close to crying. He struggled to hold back the tears.

The amplified voice boomed out again. "Mr. Shortland. We have a Jason Shortland at the desk. Shortland." As she spoke Mr. Robards put his arm around Jason's shoulders.

"Don't be afraid to cry, boy. You've earned the right. There'll be a lot of tears here tonight. They're nothing to be ashamed of." His voice was strangely shaky and Jason knew that the man who'd helped them was close to tears himself. As Jason's father ran up and took his son in his arms the tears came and Jason cried his heart out, crying on his father's shoulder.

"Dad, the house is gone. We couldn't . . . we tried . . . it was just too . . . too . . ."

"Hush, lad. Hush, hush now. It doesn't matter. We'll soon build a new house. You're here. That's all that matters. You're here. We're all safe now." He looked up. "Robards? You brought them down? Thank you. I should say more, I know, but . . . thank you."

"Nothing else to say, Tom. Good lad you've got there. Good luck." Mr. Robards turned to the doorway and was gone into the night again.

"Come on, Jason. I'll take you to your mother. She's been worried silly. Are you really all right? No burns?"

"Not really. I'm a bit singed here and there. And my clothes won't ever be much good again!" Jason tried to laugh but he didn't do a very good job of it.

CHAPTER 20

It was another two days before Shona could get back into the still-smoking and ruined township and she spent a large part of those two days worrying about her horse, Smoky. There had been terrible tales of horses being burned to death, or burned so badly they had to be humanely destroyed. She had met no one who could tell her about Smoky, or tell her whether the fire had come near the paddocks where her old friend lived.

When there had been so much human disaster she felt she had no right to worry people about her horse. There were too many other pressing problems, more important problems, but Smoky was on Shona's mind nearly all the time.

Her parents had not tried to tell her that everything would be all right, because they knew that she was intelligent enough to see the truth. The truth was that no one knew Smoky's fate.

On the day the family returned, their first stop

was Smoky's paddock. For a moment, Shona didn't dare look, then . . .

"Dad! The fire didn't even touch the paddock! There he is! He's fine! He's fine!" She was out of the car and running across the grass, the clean, sweet grass of a well-watered paddock, toward the old gray horse.

In the next paddock stood a bay horse with burns on his withers, burns that had already been dressed and treated. That horse had come out through the fire, following a truck through the smoke and flames, following a sound of a girl's voice through the blinding smoke and heat, finding his way out to the fire fighters and safety.

CHAPTER 21

Months later, the three teenagers stood in the garden of Jason's new house. His parents were having a barbecue with friends from The Avenue. There must have been twenty people around the pool. Jason knew that they included the owners of four other houses which had burned on that terrible night.

He also knew that the owners of three other burned houses were not there. They had not come back. Two other couples had moved away after the fires, too. There were many new faces in the street now. Surprised, he realized that there were more houses along The Avenue now than there had been before the fire.

"Do you still think much about the fire, Jason?" Shona's voice was quiet.

"Yes, I suppose I do. But it all seems to have happened a long time ago, doesn't it?"

"I can still remember it well enough, but only

parts of it. Like looking at a photograph album. What about you, Kristian? What do you remember about the fire?"

"Lots of things, I suppose, but they really don't fit together very well. I remember fighting for the houses. I remember Jason's house the way it was after the fire. That truck without the headlights . . . all sorts of things, but in bits and pieces."

Shona nodded. "We were too busy to store up many memories, weren't we?"

"Yes," said Jason, "but there is one thing I will always remember very clearly. It still makes me sad to think about it. I even have nightmares, sometimes . . ."

Kristian shot a quick look at Shona. "What is it, Jason? Can we ask?"

"I still remember . . . I still have nightmares about . . . about . . ." Jason looked at Shona and Kristian with anguish on his face. "I can't forget . . . that meal that Kristian cooked for us while we were waiting for the fire to come! I'll never forget that awful sludge we ate!"

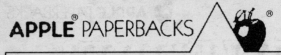

APPLE® PAPERBACKS

Pick an Apple and Polish Off Some Great Reading!

BEST-SELLING APPLE TITLES

❑ MT42975-2	**The Bullies and Me** Harriet Savitz	$2.75
❑ MT42709-1	**Christina's Ghost** Betty Ren Wright	$2.75
❑ MT41682-0	**Dear Dad, Love Laurie** Susan Beth Pfeffer	$2.75
❑ MT43461-6	**The Dollhouse Murders** Betty Ren Wright	$2.75
❑ MT42545-5	**Four Month Friend** Susan Clymer	$2.75
❑ MT43444-6	**Ghosts Beneath Our Feet** Betty Ren Wright	$2.75
❑ MT44351-8	**Help! I'm a Prisoner in the Library** Eth Clifford	$2.75
❑ MT43188-9	**The Latchkey Kids** Carol Anshaw	$2.75
❑ MT44567-7	**Leah's Song** Eth Clifford	$2.75
❑ MT43618-X	**Me and Katie (The Pest)** Ann M. Martin	$2.75
❑ MT41529-8	**My Sister, The Creep** Candice F. Ransom	$2.75
❑ MT42883-7	**Sixth Grade Can Really Kill You** Barthe DeClements	$2.75
❑ MT40409-1	**Sixth Grade Secrets** Louis Sachar	$2.75
❑ MT42882-9	**Sixth Grade Sleepover** Eve Bunting	$2.75
❑ MT41732-0	**Too Many Murphys** Colleen O'Shaughnessy McKenna	$2.75
❑ MT42326-6	**Veronica the Show-Off** Nancy K. Robinson	$2.75

Available wherever you buy books, or use this order form.

Scholastic Inc., P.O. Box 7502, 2931 East McCarty Street, Jefferson City, MO 65102

Please send me the books I have checked above. I am enclosing $_____ (please add $2.00 to cover shipping and handling). Send check or money order — no cash or C.O.D.s please.

Name ————————————————————————————

Address ————————————————————————————

City———————————————— **State/Zip** ————————————

Please allow four to six weeks for delivery. Offer good in the U.S.A. only. Sorry, mail orders are not available to residents of Canada. Prices subject to change.

APP1090